BURY ME

by
Tara Sivec

D1519694

Other books by Tara Sivec

Romantic Comedy

The Chocolate Lovers Series:

Seduction and Snacks (Chocolate Lovers #1)

Futures and Frosting (Chocolate Lovers #2)

Troubles and Treats (Chocolate Lovers #3)

The Chocoholics Series:

Love and Lists (Chocoholics #1)

Passion and Ponies (Chocoholics #2)

Tattoos and TaTas (Chocoholics #2.5)

Romantic Suspense

The Playing With Fire Series:

A Beautiful Lie (Playing With Fire #1)

Because of You (Playing With Fire #2)

Worn Me Down (Playing With Fire #3)

Closer to the Edge (Playing With Fire #4)

Romantic Suspense/Erotica

The Ignite Trilogy

Burned (Ignite Trilogy Volume 1)

Branded (Ignite Trilogy Volume 2)

Scorched (Ignite Trilogy Volume 3)

Bury Me
Copyright © 2015 Tara Sivec
Print Edition

Editing by Lisa Aurello

Cover Design by Michelle Preast
www.MichellePreast.com

Front Cover Photo by MH Photography
http://on.fb.me/1HWjMQj

Back Cover Photo by Delia D. Blackburn Photography
http://on.fb.me/1GIJN3G

Back Cover Model – Karolina Galuszynski

Interior Design by Paul Salvette, BB eBooks
bbebooksthailand.com

Prison Access/Research/Photo shoot Location – Ohio State Reformatory
www.mrps.org

For James –

Thank you for believing in me. Sorry if reading this makes you fear for your life when you fall asleep before me. Sleep with one eye open. Just kidding!

Maybe.

"All things truly wicked start from innocence."
—Ernest Hemingway

SUMMER OF 1965

PROLOGUE

I PUSH MY legs harder, my bare feet slapping against the wet earth and splashing through puddles as I weave in and out of the trees, the bright security lights around the edge of the property guiding my way into the woods. Branches and leaves smack into my face and slice across my arms, but I ignore the slashes of pain, swatting them away as I run faster. Icy rain drenches me, dripping into my eyes and a loud clap of thunder rumbles above me, but I can still hear the angry shouts not far behind.

I have to keep going. If I'm caught, I'm dead.

As I move deeper into the woods, the fluorescent lights guiding me disappear, plummeting me into profound darkness. Tripping over a tree root, I slam face first into the mud, my body shrieking in protest as pain shoots through me.

No time to hurt, no time to rest. Keep going.

Footsteps splash through the mud, getting ever closer, the voice growing more furious as threats are screamed at me. I scramble up from the muck and keep running, lightning lending brief flashes of illumination so I have some idea of where to go.

This isn't fair. I did the right thing, but no one will ever be convinced of that. Secrets never stay buried—they should have known that. So many lies, so much pain and they just DIDN'T CARE! I made things right and now I'm going to be punished for it.

"YOU WILL PAY FOR WHAT YOU DID!"

The enraged voice echoes through the woods, pushing me to keep going even though I can't catch my breath and my muscles throb with every step. The woods become denser until there's nothing but pitch black surrounding me. Lightning no longer penetrates the thick canopy and I halt in my tracks before I run smack into a tree. Holding my breath, I wait and listen, my heart hammering inside my chest.

There's no more shouting, no more pounding feet, only rain battering the trees and splashing into the muddy ground all around me. I wait it out for a few seconds.

Only quiet.

Relief washes through me. It's too dark, too muddy, too wet and too hard to find someone who will do anything to get away. My short-lived relief quickly gives way to rage. Years of pain, humiliation and scars that will never heal and just because I forced them to see the consequences of their lies, I'm going to be tossed aside once again like I'm nothing to them.

A twig snaps to my left and the adrenaline raging through my bloodstream forces me to whip around to confront the monster in the woods. My eyes strain through the darkness to discern a shape, but it's different from the one that was chasing me. Maybe I'm not going to die out here. I should be happy that I'm no longer alone in the woods with the devil at my back, but I'm not. There are always consequences to doing bad things, even if done for the right reasons.

Before I can command my feet to move toward the shape—the safer of the two evils—I hear another sound in the opposite direction and foolishly turn my head. Something heavy and solid crashes against my skull and I feel myself falling. Darkness descends over me one last time, covering my eyes, clogging my ears and stealing the breath from my lungs.

Nothing will ever be the same again.

Nothing will ever be good again.

It will all be bad.

Bad

Bad

Bad.

CHAPTER 1

"RAVENNA, IT'S GOOD to see you up and about."

I stand in the alcove that leads to the east cell block, the jangle of keys on the large brass ring my father holds as he unlocks the row of cells on the first floor echoing in the cavernous room. Strange as it sounds, my family lives in a prison. I'm sure there's a joke hidden in there somewhere considering my current mental state and the memories my mind has conveniently locked away from me, but I'm too on edge to think anything is funny. The Gallow's Hill State Penitentiary, built in 1886, is where my family has lived since my father was hired as the warden over twenty years ago. He was brought on in the middle of a high-profile class-action lawsuit filed by the prisoners claiming inhumane conditions and abuse from guards and the former warden. Even with my father's positive changes and new regulations to safeguard the prisoners, the state ruled in favor of the inmates and the Gallow's was forced to close its doors five years after he took over.

"The next tour of the facility is in thirty minutes and Ike hasn't shown up yet. How many times have you told me to fire him and get a new tour guide?"

My father chuckles as he pulls down a heavy steel lever and the entire row of rusty cell doors slowly creaks open. I wish I could laugh and share the joke with him but the truth is that I have no idea how many times I might have had this conversation with him in the past. My hand unconsciously reaches up to my forehead and the tips of my fingers graze the small bandage held there with medical tape. According to my parents and the doctor, the bump hidden beneath the white gauze is to blame for the confusion and overall uneasy feeling I've had since I woke up two days ago.

Sitting alone in my room for the last few days with nothing to occupy my time while I healed, I tried to force the memories that were buried deep in my subconscious. Scenes from my life flashed behind my eyes at random times, each one of them so fleeting and confusing that as soon as I attempted to reach out and grab one, it disappeared faster than I could take my next breath.

Stepping into the vast five-story-tall room, I walk past my father and look inside each cell as I go, wondering about all of the criminals who spent time here long ago and why my father was so intent on making us live here after the prison shut down. Having no other family to help us and no other job prospects when the prison was closed, my father convinced the state to turn the facility into a historical site and tourist attraction. We could continue to reside in the living quarters attached to the prison as long as my father agreed to manage the upkeep and run all tourist activities. With people around the world fascinated by the prison's history, as well as those who believe the tales of it being haunted, our tours are always sold out. It makes the state happy because the money this place brings in is a nice chunk for them, and it makes my father happy because we'll always have a roof over our heads, regardless of how strange the contents under the roof are.

The sound of my footsteps on the cement floor echoes around the giant room. Glancing up as I walk, the setting sun streaming in from the tall windows illuminates with an orange glow each of the five open levels that mirror the first floor. Row after row of paint-chipped cell doors stretches out in front of me as far as the eye can see. The only difference on the upper floors is the addition of metal railings to protect people from falling to their death when they walk along the narrow three-foot ledge in front of the cells. Not that it helped much back in the day, since there were plenty of reports of accidents that probably weren't accidents at all, considering why the Gallow's is no longer a working prison today. Still, the railings provide some comfort to tourists as they precariously walk the ledges of each floor and stare into the rooms where murderers and rapists spent the remainder of their days.

Stopping in front of one of the cells, I stare inside the shadowed six by eight room. Everything in the Gallow's was kept exactly as is when it was closed to add to the eeriness factor and keep tourists coming back. Some cells are in worse condition than others—everything from crumbling stone walls to holes in the floor from an attempt at fixing the plumbing—but for the most part, each cell contains a toilet, sink, and the metal frame of a bunk bed. A few even contain crude drawings, etched words of help, or slash marks indicating how many years the prior inhabitant spent inside that room. On the stone wall right above the toilet of the cell I'm standing in front of, a satanic face stares back at me, complete with horns and a forked tongue sticking out of its mouth. The words "You will pay for your sins" directly above the face makes my heart beat faster, but not in fear. Laughter bubbles up in my throat and I have to cough to hold back my abnormal reaction to the nightmarish drawing that I feel like I've stared at a hundred times before. It's etched into my brain and I can almost feel my fingers tracing over the words on the cold stone.

My father's voice breaks into my thoughts. "Are you okay, Ravenna? I can't even remember the last time you were in one of the cell blocks."

It seems odd to hear my father say he can't remember me ever being in this area. I knew that drawing was in that particular cell and I walked right up to it, knowing it would be there. There's a feeling of familiarity in here, like I've walked up and down the rows of cells thousands of times, memorizing each and every one. I drag my gaze away from the words that inspire in me an unnatural urge to laugh to watch my father walk toward me.

"Even when you gave tours, you'd stand in the doorway to give your speech and let the visitors explore on their own. You said this area gave you the creeps and you refused to walk inside."

I guess that sounds more like me. At least more like the *me* I've been told I am, instead of the one who wants to laugh in the face of Satan and his ominous message. I know I should be rubbing away goose bumps on my arms like a normal person would, staring into the small rooms where the most violent offenders in the state, going all the way back to the Civil War era, lived and died, but that's the problem. I don't feel like a normal person. I don't feel like the girl everyone keeps telling me I am.

"That's what I always loved about you," my father continues, staring blankly above us at one of the tall windows. "Even after living here all your life, you never grew immune or indifferent to this place like the rest of us. You still felt bad about the horrors that happened here before our time and they affected you deeply. You felt everything so much more keenly than anyone I've ever met."

I'm the eighteen-year-old daughter and only child of Mr. and Mrs. Tanner Duskin. My grandparents were Russian immigrants and moved their family to the United States to give them a better life when my father was just a baby. I graduated at the top of my class in high school last month and received a full ride to Brown University to study literature. I was the president of every academic club they would allow me to be and I have a very limited number of friends because someone with my extracurricular schedule didn't have time for a large group of people in her life to distract her. I wear sensible clothes that never draw attention to myself, and my long, black hair is always kept in a thick braid that trails down to the middle of my back. I have my mother's fair skin and bright green eyes and my father's serious disposition and hardworking nature. And I'm deeply affected by the things that happened in this prison, I guess.

These perfunctory facts are what I've been told about myself the last few days when I woke up in a state of confusion from a two-day coma. They are the list of my attributes, given to me by my mother as if she were reciting a grocery list.

"We need eggs, milk and bread. You have my eyes, a good head on your shoulders and you're the most perfect daughter anyone could ever ask for."

This is the reason why I've stopped asking questions and I pretend as if nothing is amiss in my addled brain. These are the facts I've been told and the only truths anyone will give me about myself. This is the girl my parents raised and the girl they pinned all of their hopes and dreams on.

This is also the girl my father speaks about in past tense, as if she doesn't exist anymore, even though I'm standing within touching distance of him.

"I think I'm going to head back up to my room before anyone gets here," I tell my father, keeping my eyes focused on him, instead of back inside the cell where they want to go.

"That's probably a good idea. You've had a rough couple of days."

He turns away from the window and opens his arms to me. I hesitate for a moment before walking into them. When I do, I bury my face in the lapels of his black suit coat and inhale his scent: peppermint from the mints he always keeps in the inside pocket of his coat and the faint, fruity smoke from the pipe he sneaks when my mother isn't at home, and the reason for the peppermints.

My father is a tall man and my cheek barely

reaches his chest as I wrap my arms around his waist. Eighteen years of hugs, eighteen years of comfort and yet it feels like this is the first time he's ever held me this tightly.

A wave of uneasiness suddenly washes over me and instead of feeling comfort in my father's arms, I feel trapped and claustrophobic. I quickly pull myself out of his embrace and back away from him. He looks down at me sadly, his arms still held open from my quick departure. I force a small smile on my face before turning and walking quickly through the door to take me away from the cell block. Once I'm out of my father's view, I pick up the pace and jog through the rooms and hallways that intersect, leading me away from the main area of the prison and toward the lobby where I can then take the stairs up to our living quarters. I pass the guard stations, prison showers, and administrative offices as I go, all of them empty with peeling paint on the walls, cobwebs, and a quiet eeriness about them. I know the way through these halls like the back of my hand and I can recite the history and violent acts that happened in each room, but I can't explain why I woke up covered in bruises and scratches, with a headache that, two days later, still rages behind my eyes.

Turning the last corner that will take me into the main hallway by the front doors and gift shop, my body slams into something solid and I stumble backward. Strong hands wrap around my upper arms, jerking me forward before I can fall on my ass. Glancing up quickly, I peer into a set of beautiful pale blue eyes. They mesmerize me for a few seconds until the hands gripping my arms suddenly push me away. I stare at the man standing in front of me, feeling a spark of familiarity when I look at him. He looks to be in his twenties and is wearing faded jeans and an old band t-shirt covered in specks of dirt. His blonde hair is cut short on the sides and longer on top, a few shaggy tufts falling down over one eye as he looks at me. Even with a thick lock of hair obscuring some of his face, I can still see his eyes narrow in annoyance at me.

"You should watch where you're going, Ravenna. You can't afford any more *accidents*."

I feel my face heat at his words and know my pale skin is turning red. He obviously knows who I am, but the angry look on his face as he glares at me makes me wonder if it's a good idea for me to know *him*.

My heart starts beating rapidly as he continues to stare at me without saying another word. I feel a shiver run through my body and goose bumps break out on my arms. All the things I was supposed to feel over in the cell block have suddenly manifested just from the look this guy is giving me, and I'm frozen in fear. The bump on my head suddenly starts to ache and I have a quick image of running through the woods in the middle of the night, covered in rain and mud. I gasp out loud, but just as soon as I try to reach into my mind to grab more of the memory, it disappears in a flash and my brain shuts down.

"Nolan, what are you doing in here?"

I jump when I hear my father's angry voice behind me and pull my gaze away from the man in front of me to turn my head. My father stands in the hallway with his hands on his hips and one eyebrow raised questioningly.

"Just bringing in some fresh flowers, like you asked. There's a vase next to the register in the gift shop and one in the artifact room."

My father nods, folding his arms in front of him. "Then there's no need for you to be dallying inside. The grounds around the lake need to be mowed today."

Nolan's arm brushes against mine as he moves around me to head toward my father, bringing forth a whole new round of goose bumps. My father steps out of the way to let him exit through the huge twelve-foot-tall wooden door that leads outside. They share a quiet look as Nolan passes, stepping out onto the front porch before the heavy door slams closed.

When we're alone in the hallway, my father sighs deeply before turning to look at me.

"Who was that guy?" I ask, rubbing the coldness from my arms.

"You don't remember Nolan?"

I shake my head and my father shoves his hands

into the front pockets of his black suit pants, his face displaying a flash of relief at my reply, which makes me want to ask a hundred questions. All of which I'm sure won't be answered in the way I need.

"That's just as well you don't remember. His name is Nolan Michaels and he's been a groundskeeper here for almost two years. He has some…issues, and you've always been very good at listening to me when I've told you to stay away from him. I trust you'll keep that in mind while you're recovering?"

He makes it sound like he's asking, but I can tell by the tone of his voice that he's just doing it to be polite and this is a command I should heed. I don't really appreciate being told who I can and can't talk to, especially when I have so many questions and so many holes in my memory that neither he nor my mother is willing to fill with anything useful. If Nolan has known me for two years, even if I was never allowed to associate with him, he's got to know something about what happened.

According to the doctor, my parents being vague and not filling my head with *their* opinions about what happened will help me come to the truth on my own. It's like pulling teeth to get either one of them to disclose information to me so the idea that there might be an outside party who can shed some light on things fills me with excitement, even if my first instinct with Nolan was to run the other way.

The doorbell chimes through the hallway, indicating the first of the tourists have arrived. With my piercing headache growing stronger the longer I try to make sense of things in my head, I turn and unhook the heavy satin rope blocking the stairs that lead up to our living quarters, quickly reattaching it and racing up the stairs as loud voices fill the hallway while my father greets the tour group.

At the top of the stairs, I walk through the living room, glancing around at the five outer rooms that surround this central location—my parents' bedroom, my father's office, a kitchen, spare bedroom and finally, my room. Standing in the doorway of my room, I stare at the pink blanket draped over my bed and the pink paint covering my walls. I lift my chin in determination, stomp over to my bed and rip the blanket from the top. I do the same with the matching sheets and pillowcases until there's a large pile of cotton-blend bedding in the corner of my bedroom that resembles a fluffy pink cloud. I hate the color pink, but going by what my mother has told me, and the cotton-candy hue everywhere I look, it's been my favorite color since I was born.

Throwing myself down on the stripped bed, I stare up at my ceiling and wonder if I have the guts to approach Nolan and ask him some questions. When I cross my arms over my chest I wince when my palms press against the area on my upper arms where he grabbed me when I bumped into him. Unfolding my arms, I hold one out in front of me, tracing the faint red marks that his fingers made against the pale skin of my bicep. My fingers trail down my arm to my wrist, over the bruises that have been there since I woke up two days ago and are just now starting to fade from angry purple to yellow. They're the exact same size and shape as the marks on my upper arm and I quickly drop my hands to the mattress and take a few deep breaths.

I softly begin to chant the things I'm supposed to believe are true.

"My name is Ravenna Duskin. I'm eighteen years old and I live in a prison. I love the color pink and my parents would never lie to me. My name is Ravenna Duskin. I'm eighteen years old and I live in a prison. I love the color pink and my parents would never lie to me."

I whisper these words over and over until I can't ignore the exhaustion that overwhelms me and my eyelids grow heavy with sleep, my room filling with shadows as the sun sets in the distance. I let my eyes drift closed and try not to fear the darkness behind my lids.

"My name is Ravenna Duskin. I'm eighteen years old and I live in a prison…"

CHAPTER 2

"T HIS HURTS ME as much as it does you. Just calm down and it will be over soon."

The voice fills me with rage, but before I can vent my hatred, an excruciating jolt shoots through my body, bowing my back and paralyzing my legs. The pain is so intense that I want to cry, but I will never show that kind of weakness. I focus on the sound of the zapping electricity filling the room, imagining all the ways I'll get my revenge some day very soon.

Silence suddenly fills the room and my body collapses back down onto the table, tremors shaking through it with the aftereffects of the shock.

"If you'd learn to control your urges, I wouldn't have to do this to you."

I stare with hatred at the face leaning over me, wishing there weren't leather straps holding my arms and legs down so I could wrap my hands around that skinny neck and squeeze and squeeze until the life drained out of those cold, dark eyes.

"I know you hate me, but this is for your own good. You have to stop being so bad."

I've heard these words so many times over the years that they mean nothing to me. I can't stop the way I am. I can't stop the way I feel. No matter what's done to me, nothing will change who I am.

"Will you stop being bad?"

My eyes narrow and I focus every atom of hatred I can at the face above me, unable to speak with the plastic guard in my mouth.

A deep sigh fills the room. "So be it."

I bite down harder on the plastic in my mouth and refuse to close my eyes as the dial is turned up a notch and humming starts to fill the room. Every time this is done to me, I have to listen to the humming of that damn song. The song from my childhood that always used to calm me down now just fills me with rage.

The crackling and whirring of the rise in power makes the lights flicker above my head and the button is pressed once again. Even though I'm ready for the pain, it still takes my breath away when it zaps through my body. Everything from the top of my head to the tips of my toes ignites in agony like I'm being set on fire from the inside out. My body jerks and convulses, rattling against the metal table beneath me. No matter how hard I try to fight through it, flashes of light flicker behind my eyes until I see nothing but darkness as I collapse back down on the table, my final thoughts of pain, torture, and death. Not my own, though. These thoughts are solely for the people who did this to me.

Every one of them.

I bolt up in bed, a loud, piercing scream filling the room and I realize it's coming from me. Clamping a hand over my mouth to silence myself, I look around frantically, trying to remember where I am and what woke me up. My heart thunders in my chest as the sun's bright rays shine through my window and directly onto my bed, warming my chilled body. The remnants of my dream vanish before I can pin any down to remember. Looking down at myself, I realize I'm wearing the same clothes as last night, but they're now thick with cold sweat and sticking to my body.

As I swing my legs over the side of my bed, my door suddenly opens and my mother stands in the doorway with a worried look on her face. Her hair, once as pitch black as mine, is streaked with grey and pulled back from her face in a low, messy bun. Judging by the pale blue housecoat with tiny pink flowers she wears atop her nightgown that is buttoned all askew, I'm assuming I woke her up with my screams and she hastily threw it on to come to me.

"Ravenna, are you okay? I thought I heard you

scream."

Her soft voice brings tears to my eyes as I gaze across the room at her, looking at me with so much love and concern. As I blink back the tears and swallow the thick lump in my throat, she rushes to the bed and sits down next to me. Her arm wraps around my back and she pulls me against her, using her free hand to gently pull my head down to her shoulder. She rocks us slowly back and forth and right when I start to close my eyes and relax, she begins to hum. After the first verse, the humming changes to the words that go along with the melody.

"The monkey thought 'twas all in fun, pop goes the weasel."

Her softly sung words fill me with a burst of anger I don't understand. I clench my hands into fists in my lap, the bite of pain as my nails dig into my palms pushing away the sudden urge to wrap my hands around her neck and squeeze as hard as I can.

What is happening to me? What the hell is happening?

Scrambling away from her, I bolt from my bed and rush to the other side of my room where my dresser is. Refusing to turn around and look at her, I yank open my drawers to grab some clean clothes.

"I'm going to take a shower," I explain in a rush, clutching my clothes to my chest and hurrying into the small bathroom attached to my room. I scurry around the door, using my back to push it closed behind me. When I'm alone, I let out a relieved breath and drop my clothes onto the tile at my feet. Not wanting to dwell on what just happened in my bedroom, I move across the room and turn on the shower, hoping the hot water will wash away all of the uneasy thoughts and strange feelings coursing through me.

When I emerge from the shower fifteen minutes later, I feel lighter and more at ease as I wrap my towel around me and open the bathroom door. Steam billows out around me as I step off of the bathroom tile and onto the hardwood in my room. I jump in surprise when I see my mother still sitting on the bed where I left her. She turns away from me for a moment and I see her quickly swipe at the tears I noticed on her cheeks when I walked into the room. When she turns back around, she's all smiles as she pats the bed next to her and holds up the brush she has in the other hand.

"Sit down and I'll braid your hair."

My feet move robotically across the room and I clutch the towel tighter to my body as I ease down next to her and give her my back. As she runs the brush through my hair and starts gathering pieces at the top of my head to start the braid, I close my eyes and let the feel of her fingers sliding through my wet hair soothe me. When she's finished and has the ends secured with a hair band, she pats my shoulder and I feel the bed dip as she gets up. I get up with her and walk over to the mirror above my dresser to stare at my reflection. My mother comes up behind me and rests her hands on my bare shoulders. I hate having my hair pulled back, but I haven't voiced this to her for some reason. It's too tight and it makes my head ache, but each morning since I woke up disoriented, my mother has come into my room and insisted this is how I've always worn my hair. I do as she says, since everyone tells me I need to get back into my daily routine from before the accident, but I can't stand the sight in front of me.

"You look beautiful," she tells me with a smile, as I continue to stare at the girl in the mirror who I barely recognize.

"I hate my hair like this," I suddenly admit to her with a burst of confidence.

Her smile falters for just a moment before it's back, bigger and brighter than ever. "Nonsense. You hate having your hair in your face. I've braided your hair every morning since you were a little girl. It's how a proper young woman *should* look.

My recent thoughts of wanting to do her harm make me feel anything but proper.

She turns away from me and walks toward the door as I continue staring at my reflection, wanting to rip the band out of the braid and claw at my hair until it's a tangled mess around my face.

"Oh, I almost forgot," my mother adds as she stops in the doorway. Trudy is stopping by to check on you today."

I turn and stare at her blankly and she bites her lower lip worriedly.

"You remember Trudy, right?"

Trudy Marshall: eighteen years old, blonde hair, and my friend since elementary school.

Giving my mother a cheerful smile, I nod. "Of course I remember Trudy."

I hate Trudy. She's a snobby bitch who thinks she's better than me and wants to take what's mine.

The mean thought in my head makes my smile falter, but I put it right back in place so my mother will stop looking at me like I'm crazy. Trudy is my friend. She's one of my only friends and she's never thought it was weird that I lived in a prison, like so many others. I have no idea where that errant thought came from and I don't like it.

"She's been so worried about you," my mother continues. "She wanted to come sooner but your father wouldn't let anyone visit for a few days so you could rest. Why don't you put on a nice dress and I'll make the two of you some fresh lemonade and sandwiches for lunch?"

I nod distractedly as she gently closes the door behind her and leaves me alone.

I should be excited that someone is coming to visit after feeling so alone the last few days, but something about Trudy leaves me feeling strangely angry about seeing her. My mind is at war with the facts about her that are engrained into my head and a fleeting thought that there's a reason I don't like her. Just like every other thought in my head, it doesn't stick around long enough for me to grab onto and examine it.

Scrubbing my palms up and down my face in frustration, I sigh loudly and walk over to my closet to find something to wear. The metallic screech of the hangers, sliding across the clothing rod as I flip through one ugly dress after another, fills the room. Half of the dresses are different shades of pink, the other half are varying pastels; they are all boring and more fit for a fifty-year-old woman than a teenager. Yanking the least offending one off of the hanger before I try to find a pair of scissors and cut everything in this closet to shreds, I hold the pale yellow dress up in front of me and glare at it. With a defeated shake of my head, I drop my towel and begin getting dressed.

When I woke up in this room three days ago, I felt like I didn't belong in it, even though the room was familiar and I knew it was mine. I stared at my mother and father standing by my bedside with worried looks on their faces and even though I knew who they were, deep down inside they felt like strangers. When the doctor asked me what year it was, I knew it was 1965. I knew I was eighteen and I knew before I looked in the mirror that I had long black hair, green eyes, and a slim build. I knew the answer to every question he asked me about the prison and my parents, but I faltered when asked about the gash on my head and the scratches and bruises on my arms. When I started to panic and demand answers about what happened to me, I was told not to worry and that the important thing was that I was safe and my injuries would heal. No one seemed to understand that I didn't care about the superficial cuts on my arms, the scrapes on my legs, and the bump on my head. I knew those would heal in time. What I cared about, what no one seemed to be in a hurry to help me with, was the injury inside my own mind.

I keep telling myself it's only been three days. Three short days after something happened to me that no one wanted to talk about. A part of me wonders if everyone around me is lying and they know what happened. That it's so horrific I'm better off not knowing. I know it's supposed to take time and three days isn't much in the grand scheme of things, but as each day passes, I get more and more confused and feel like everything I know is a lie. Nothing is falling into place and everything feels wrong.

It's hard to believe that three days ago, in the middle of the night during a thunderstorm, I was out in the woods at the edge of the property alone. My parents say they don't know why I was out there. They don't know what happened that caused me to get hurt and forget bits and pieces of my memories. I'm a good girl, they tell me. I'm a proper girl who wears proper dresses, and a proper hairstyle, but a good girl doesn't go wandering alone in the woods at night unless she's asking for trouble.

A good girl doesn't think of harming her mother.

A good girl doesn't want to rip the perfectly constructed braid from her head and scream at the reflection in the mirror.

A good girl doesn't want to slash all of the clothes in her closet because they look nothing like something she would ever wear.

"My name is Ravenna Duskin. I'm eighteen years old and I live in a prison," I recite to myself as I slip on a pair of shoes and head out of my bedroom.

CHAPTER 3

OUR LIVING QUARTERS at Gallow's Hill are pretty small compared to a normal home, but in the grand scheme of things, the entire six-building facility and the 150 acres surrounding it are technically considered our home as well and this small area is only where we eat and sleep. It's like living in our own little town.

The living room and four rooms attached have been here since the building was first constructed. Wardens and their families always lived on-site of the prison due to the fact of it being located so far from any major city or town. Back in the early days when there weren't any cars or other faster means of transportation, if an emergency at the prison arose in the middle of the night, it was easier to have the warden here at all times to attend to it, instead of waiting for the time it would take to get him here. In the early days, guards and other employees were tasked with making sure the warden's family had everything they needed to live comfortably, so the family never had to leave for such things as groceries or other supplies. For the first few years of my life when Gallow's Hill was still a working prison, my father would send the guards out for birthday decorations, Christmas presents, school supplies, and anything else we ever wanted or needed. It was like having our own personal butlers to do our bidding and we became very spoiled. After the prison closed its doors and was turned into a historical building, we no longer had anyone to wait on us hand and foot and my mother was put in charge of running all the errands, and then it fell to me when I was able to drive.

Still, Gallow's Hill remained our own private town, so to speak, and we have everything we need to survive here, leaving little need or want for us to ever leave. Aside from the tours and random charity events held here, our family keeps to themselves for the most part.

Walking in a circle around the living room, I stare at photos of our family that hang on the walls. There are smiles on our faces in each photo, but none of them seem real. None of those smiles reach our eyes, and it makes me wonder just how happy we really could have been living here all these years alone, so far from the closest town and so far from other people. I was homeschooled until high school when my mother thought it was a good idea that I meet other kids and get away from the seclusion of the prison. I only had Trudy as a friend for so long because her father used to work here as a guard-turned-tour guide. My mother made friends with Mrs. Marshall when she would bring her husband his lunch back then, and since they both had daughters the same age, and my mother finally found someone she had something in common with, we all became friends.

I stop in front of a framed photo resting on the mantel of the small stone fireplace in the corner of the room. It's a black and white photo of my parents and I, taken when I was five years old. It's the only photo in the room where none of us have fake smiles on our faces. I'm staring off at something in the distance, not even looking at the camera. My father looks stern and rigid, and my mother looks like a strong wind will knock her over. Her face is gaunt and the area around her eyes is puffy. If the photo were in color, I'm wondering if I would see redness around her eyes from crying. I don't understand why this photo, so depressing and unlike the rest in the room, is sitting on the mantel on display for everyone to see each time they walk into this room. I know I was only five when this photo was taken, but I can remember that day very clearly in my head. A storm was coming and there were dark clouds overhead. I was angry at the time, filled with rage that a normal five-year-old should never feel. I can hear myself screaming at someone, strong arms wrapped around my small body, dragging me into the picture as I kicked and clawed and tried to get away. I hated everyone around me, and I hated being forced to do something I didn't want to do. The rage and the unhappiness flow through me as I stare at the photo, and I want to rip it down from the mantel, throw it to the floor and smash it into a thousand pieces. I want to stomp my feet on top of the photo and grind the shards of glass into my parents' faces until they are scratched and distorted and ruined.

I want to ruin them the same way they ruined me.

My hands shake with anger as I lift my arm toward the photo. I see splotches of red at the edges of my vision as my hand wraps around the metal frame, and I grip it so hard my knuckles turn white.

"So you ARE alive."

I jump, letting go of the photo guiltily when a voice penetrates the fog of my memories. Quickly turning around, I see Trudy standing at the top of the stairs wearing a pair of bell-bottom jeans and a frilly pink button-down shirt.

"Why wouldn't I be alive?" I ask her in confusion.

She laughs and rolls her eyes at me, moving farther into the room to flop down on the couch, pulling her feet under her legs.

"It was a joke, Ravenna, lighten up," she says with another laugh. "I haven't seen you in three days, and every time I've called to check up on you and ask about coming over, your father has practically bitten my head off and told me to stay away."

Moving away from the fireplace, I take a seat next to her on the couch.

"I thought maybe you died or something, and

your family was trying to keep it a secret," she says with another laugh.

I'm not really sure why the idea that I might have died and my family tried to cover it up is funny, but before I can ask about that, something she said hits me like a brick.

"You said you haven't seen me in three days. So you saw me the day I got hurt? You were here?" I question.

If Trudy was here that day, she knows something. She'll be able to fill in the missing pieces so my brain doesn't feel like Swiss cheese.

Trudy stares at me for a few minutes, and her mouth drops open in shock.

"Holy shit," she whispers. I thought your mom was kidding when she told me you didn't remember anything when she let me in downstairs. You really don't remember what happened?"

I feel embarrassment heat up my face and I shake my head.

Trudy whistles and cocks her head to the side as she studies me. "So weird. You look like crap, by the way."

It's my turn to roll my eyes at her. "Thanks a lot."

The way she has her head tilted to the side has moved her curtain of blonde hair away from one side of her neck. I lean toward her a little closer when I see what looks like scratches on her skin. They are long and deep and disappear into the collar of her shirt.

"What happened to your neck?"

Trudy's hand flies up to the side of her neck, and she covers up the scratches, laughing sheepishly.

"Oh, it's nothing. I'm guessing you forgot about the kitten my mom got me for a graduation present?" she asks, nervously pulling her long hair forward to drape over her shoulders, effectively hiding the marks from me.

I look into her eyes, knowing without a doubt that she's lying to me, but I have no idea why.

"I asked for a car, and I got a kitten," she huffs in annoyance. "How in the hell is a kitten going to help me get to and from college in the fall? Anyway, that little ball of fur hates me. Every time I pick her up she scratches me.

"So… back to you," she says with a smile, changing the subject. "You really don't remember anything?"

I'm so sick and tired of feeling like people are lying to me. Why won't anyone tell me the truth?

"Why were you here three days ago?" I fire back.

Trudy swallows nervously and fiddles with one of the cuff buttons on her blouse. "We were just going to hang out. You know, talk about college and stuff, no big deal. You invited me over, but when you answered the door you were acting really weird."

"Weird how?" I ask.

Trudy shrugs. "I don't know, just weird. You were dressed differently, your hair was all wild and crazy, and, to be honest, you were kind of mean to me."

My hand reaches up to touch the braid at the back of my head, once again feeling the urge to rip it out and let my long black hair fall down my back, free of the tight constriction.

"You called me all sorts of names and told me to go home. I didn't even realize you *knew* words like that until you shouted them at me," she says with an uncomfortable laugh, trying to lighten the mood.

"You're just like every other whore, trying to take what isn't yours. No one is falling for that innocent act you put on, you snobby, lying bitch."

In a quick flash, I can see myself clear as day, standing on the front porch of the prison, the thunder and lightning echoing all around as I shout angry words at someone who is supposed to be my friend. Words that don't match the petite, smiling blonde sitting in front of me, but words I feel deep down inside are true.

"It's no big deal; I've already forgiven you," she tells me with an easy smile. "It's pretty obvious you weren't in your right state of mind that night for whatever reason. I'm just glad you're okay. You seem like you're back to your old self and that's all that matters, right?"

It's not all that matters, not by a long shot. It's pretty obvious she's not telling me everything. Aside from the fact that I acted and looked different that night, why was I so angry with her? What would have made me so enraged that I would shout such nasty things at someone who is supposed to be my friend?

"Do you know the guy who works here? Nolan?" I ask her, trying one last time to see if she'll be honest about something.

Her smile immediately falls and she pulls her legs out from under her, shifting her body nervously on the couch.

"Stay away from that guy; he's bad news," she warns me.

I already got that message from my father and the overall uneasy feeling I had around him made me agree, but it's clear that I can't trust anything Trudy tells me.

"Why is he bad news? What has he done?"

She pushes herself up from the couch and lets out a stilted laugh. "He's just not a good guy, okay? I don't even know why your father lets him work here. I mean, he's cute and all and nice to look at, but there's something off with him. I don't know him personally or anything, but it's what I've heard. Stay away from him, okay?"

Trudy moves around my legs and heads for the stairs. "I have to get going; my mom wants to go shopping for college stuff."

I quickly stand and follow her toward the stairs. "My mom was going to make us lunch. Don't you want to stay?"

She thumps down the stairs at a hurried pace, and I follow behind her. I don't really want to spend more time with her when she's not going to honestly answer the questions I have for her, but she was here the night everything happened. She's the key to unlocking my memories, and I have to do whatever I can to open that lock if I want to find out what happened.

I follow her down the hallway toward the front door.

"Tell your mom thanks. Maybe another time," she says as she reaches for the handle of the door.

It suddenly opens before she can get to it, and I stop a few feet behind her as she jumps out of the way.

I watch as Nolan steps inside, a surprised look on his face as his glance shifts between Trudy and me before focusing on her.

"Nice to see you again, Trudy," he tells her with a cocky smile.

Her face immediately reddens in embarrassment, and she gives him a wide berth as she quickly moves around him and out the front door. Nolan turns and watches her leave as she yells over her shoulder without turning around.

"I'll give you a call later to see how you're doing, Ravenna."

She jogs down the stairs of the front porch and disappears from sight. When she's gone, Nolan turns back around and stares at me silently. Trudy was right: he really is something nice to look at, even if being alone with him right now makes me nervous. His skin is tanned from working outside all day, and the finely toned muscles in his arms and under his t-shirt prove that he spends most of his time doing a lot of hard manual labor. He's taller than me and obviously stronger.

Strong enough to hurt me if he wanted to.

Trudy told me he was bad news and at least that information feels right for some reason, but she also said she didn't know him personally. Going by the familiar way Nolan looked at her and said her name, he knows her, and she definitely knows him.

"Tell your father I finished mowing around the lake, and I'm going to head home for the day," he tells me gruffly.

Without waiting for a reply, he backs out of the door, and it slams closed behind him. My feet stay glued to their spot in the middle of the hallway as I stare at the large wooden door.

"My name is Ravenna Duskin. I'm eighteen years old, I live in a prison, and my best friend is lying to me."

CHAPTER 4

I SPEND THE next few days wandering around the inside of Gallow's Hill, reciting facts about the prison to myself as I go, hoping the things I know will unlock some of the things I don't, but nothing works. I feel like I do when I sometimes fill in for my father as tour guide, saying things I've memorized from a book instead of things I should inherently know after growing up here.

I've attempted to get some fresh air and walk the grounds outside a few times these last couple of days, but each time I've stepped out onto the porch, I've seen Nolan working around the yard. Even if his back is to me, he immediately stops what he's doing as if he somehow senses I'm close. When he turns and looks at me and our eyes meet, I'm immediately filled with fear, and I rush back inside, pushing aside the need for fresh air and sunshine to run away from the man who looks at me with equal parts anger and curiosity.

While my days are filled with wandering and trying to avoid Nolan, my evenings are filled with uncomfortable dinners with my parents at the small kitchen table in our living quarters. With stilted conversation and vague answers to the questions I ask, I feel like I'm sitting at a table surrounded by strangers instead of the people who raised and love me.

Needing something to do to occupy myself, I've spent the last hour rearranging items in the gift shop and stacking new inventory on the metal shelves that take up most of the small room. I suddenly hear raised voices upstairs, and I pause with a folded t-shirt in my hands, craning my neck to better hear. A loud thump above my head has me tossing the shirt haphazardly on top of a pile of others and moving quickly out of the room toward the stairs. I tiptoe upwards, careful to avoid the loose floorboards, so the creak from the old wood doesn't alert anyone to my presence. At the top of the stairs I pause as the voices grow louder, and I hold my breath as I listen to my parents argue.

"There's something not right with her, Tanner; you've got to see that," my mother complains.

I hear the shuffling of feet and I move a little closer to their closed bedroom door.

"Stop borrowing trouble, Claudia. Just keep reminding her who she is and everything will be fine," my father tells her in an irritated voice.

"We shouldn't have to *remind* her who she is!" my mother shouts. "We shouldn't have to tell her what kind of person she is! She's not the same person, and I know it. I know what you did, Tanner. No matter what lies you keep telling me, I know what you did! What happened to my baby? What the hell did you do with my baby?! Where did *she* go?"

A loud smack echoes from behind the door, and I jump when I hear my mother's loud gasp of surprise and whimper of pain.

"I did what I had to do to keep this family safe, just like I did eighteen years ago. That girl downstairs is Ravenna. She's the same good, beautiful, perfect daughter we've raised her entire life. I will not let you ruin this family as you tried to do once before. Ravenna is going to be fine as long as you keep your stupid theories to yourself."

I hear footsteps stomping toward the door, and I race across the living room, dashing into my bedroom just as my parents' door swings open. Hiding behind my door, I peek out and watch my father storm through the living room and head downstairs. With a few deep breaths to calm my thumping heart, I wait a few minutes before leaving the comfort of my room, giving myself enough time so my mother doesn't know I heard what they were saying. When I get to my parents' bedroom doorway, I find my mother sitting on the edge of her bed, wiping tears from her cheeks.

"What's wrong?" I ask her in concern, even though I know she won't tell me the truth.

She looks up in surprise and plasters on a fake smile. "Ravenna, I didn't know you were here. I thought you were going for a walk around the prison."

Quickly standing, my mother hurries over to the closet, keeping her back to me to hide the misery on her face.

"I was, but I got hungry, so I was going to get a snack from the kitchen," I lie.

She reaches up to the top shelf of her closet and pulls down one of the many hatboxes stored up there, and I realize she was getting ready to run errands before the argument with my father, judging by the pale blue A-line double-breasted suit jacket and matching knee-length skirt she's currently wearing. My mother never leaves the prison without dressing properly in a designer suit with matching pillbox hat, white gloves, and pearls. With the hatbox in her hand, she moves back to the bed and sets it on top, lifting the lid to remove the sky blue hat nestled inside.

"I'm heading out to pick up some groceries, but I could fix you a snack before I leave," she tells me as she sets the hat on top of her head and pins it in place.

"No, that's okay. Why were you crying?" I ask, trying to bring her focus back to the original issue.

Pulling a pair of white gloves out of the hatbox, she slides them on her slender hands and then walks over to me as I lean against the doorframe. She brings her satin-covered hands up to my face and cups my cheeks in her palms. She stares deeply into my eyes and within seconds I feel uncomfortable, wanting to pull away, run from the room and hide, so she can't look at me like she's trying to figure out who I am. I don't want her to see; I don't want her to know and the longer she looks, the more she'll be convinced that the words she spoke to my father have some truth to them, and there really is something wrong with me.

"Don't worry about me, Ravenna; I'm fine," she tells me softly. "Just another stressful day at Gallow's Hill, nothing new."

She chuckles to give the words lightheartedness, instead of the deeper meaning I know is there.

"I love you, Ravenna," she whispers. "You're a good girl, and I love you so much."

I should be comforted by her words, but they fill me with panic. I feel like she's only saying this to me because of my father's threat to her. She's reminding me who I am to convince herself that everything is fine. That *I'm* fine and I'm normal, and I'm the same girl she's raised and loved. I feel like I've been craving these words from her forever and that I would do anything to hear them, but it doesn't make sense. She's my mother, and she loves me. Hearing her tell me this shouldn't come as a surprise, and I shouldn't feel like I don't deserve her love or her kindness.

My mother runs one gloved hand down over the top of my head and gives me a sad smile before moving around me and leaving the room. As I listen to her heels click against the hardwood floor as she walks through the living room and down the stairs, I close my eyes and let my head thump back against the frame of the door.

"My name is Ravenna Duskin. I'm eighteen years old, I live in a prison, and my parents are lying to me."

CHAPTER 5

M Y BODY GLIDES *easily through the water, my legs kicking harder to push me closer to the wall. Tilting my head to the side on the surface, I take one last huge breath before diving under, flipping over and pushing off the cement side with my feet to send me soaring in the opposite direction.*

My muscles ache with each lap I swim, but it's a pain I welcome. It reminds me I'm alive, I'm still fighting, and I'm getting stronger, as opposed to the agony I'm forced to endure on a regular basis.

This is my treat for being good. This is my reward for doing as I'm asked and never questioning the things that are done to me. My lungs are on fire as I push and pull my arms through the cold water, but I don't care. This is the only place I feel in control of my life. I'm so tired of the tests that I'm never going to pass and the pain inflicted on me in the hopes that it will change everything about me. I'm never going to change. I'm never going to be a different person. I was born this way, I will stay this way, and I will make them pay for what they've done to me.

Stepping down off of the sprawling front porch that wraps around the entire front section of the east wing of the prison, I take a minute to stare up at the front of the huge stone structure. Made out of its original brick and mortar, it's quite obvious that Gallow's Hill is a very old building constructed a very long time ago, with its Victorian Gothic style and pointed turrets on top of each guard tower. The building has remained in surprisingly good condition on the outside, needing only a few repairs here and there to fix a leak in the roof or wayward crumbling bricks. Since the prison relies on grants from the state in order to make any type of repairs, only the most detrimental ones are fixed immediately, the ones that would prevent us from conducting tours. As long as the peeling paint, crumbling stones inside the cell blocks, and loose floorboards throughout the prison add to the creepy factor of the tours and don't pose a threat to any visitors, they are pushed aside for more effective ways to spend the small amount of money the state gives us to run the facility.

Aside from the retelling of true events that have happened here and the invention of completely outrageous myths that people buy into, the building itself is one of the main draws for tourists. It's huge and ominous, even in daytime. Pulling up the long, winding driveway and getting a first glimpse of it through the trees makes visitors feel like they're starring in their very own horror movie. At least that's what all of the tourists say. To me, this place is just home. It's where I was born, where I grew up, and where I celebrated birthdays and holidays. We had family picnics on the lawn during summer days and caught lightning bugs in mason jars when the sun went down. It all sounds so perfect and idyllic as I stand here thinking about it, but something tugs at the back of my mind making me question the things I know. How can we be such a perfect, normal family after the way my father spoke to my mother yesterday? How can I have all these wonderful, happy thoughts in my head, but at the same time see a photo in our living room that makes me want to scream that everything I know is a lie?

After an hour of staring out my bedroom window and not seeing any sign of people working around the grounds today, I quickly dressed and hoped my instincts were right and that Nolan isn't here today. I'm tired of the cloying, musty scent of the prison walls. I'm tired of the dreary darkness of being stuck inside, and I'm tired of being afraid to go anywhere just because of one guy. This is my home and I'm not going to allow him to make me feel fearful anymore.

Turning away from the building, I make my way down the sidewalk and around the side of the building, headed toward the lake located about an acre away.

With my face turned up toward the sun, I let it warm me as I make my way down to the lake. I let the chirping of birds and the soft breeze that rustles the leaves in the trees take my mind off of my troubles. Regardless of the fact that the 150 acres of land surrounding the prison used to be a place for inmates to farm and be forced to work relentlessly under the boiling sun all day long in penance for their sins, it's still a beautiful area. Filled with rolling hills and lush green grass as far as the eye can see, it now resembles acres and acres of a park-like setting, instead of a prison farm. Gone are the fields of soybeans and corn the inmates were tasked with cultivating day in and day out. When the prison was shut down, my father let everything grow over, no longer having the benefit of a few hundred workers to keep things going. I like it much better like this, where I can roam the grounds alone without having an escort because when the prison was open, there were shackled inmates everywhere who could pose a threat at any moment, not that I could remember such a time.

Walking down to the lake means I have to pass

the small cemetery on the property, an area that I've always avoided for as long as I can remember. Even as I quicken my pace when I walk by the half-acre area surrounded by a low stone wall, I feel drawn to it in a strange way. Part of me knows that I've never set foot inside those stone walls. The idea of having people buried on this land, knowing they died inside the prison and had no family who cared about them enough to take them elsewhere to spend eternity has always given me the chills. Another part of me, the part that doesn't believe half of the memories I have and questions everything I remember, can see myself clearly wandering through the old and broken head-stones, memorizing all of the information and running my hands over the cold cement markers. I can feel the grass beneath my back as I rest on top of a grave with my hands beneath my head and my legs crossed at the ankles.

Soon, there will be a few more graves added to this spot. They will rot and decay and writhe in agony when they show up at the gates of hell, just like they deserve.

My feet stutter to a stop right at the entrance to the cemetery when I'm hit with that thought, so vicious and unsettling that I have to press my hand over my mouth to keep the contents of my lunch in my stomach. My eyes dart back and forth over the tops of the stone crosses and other markers I can see through the opening into the cemetery. I don't like this place. I don't like being reminded that people died in the place that I call home, even if it happened long before I was born. My mind is just playing tricks on me—it has to be. I'm not a mean person and I would never wish harm on someone else. I'm a good girl, a good daughter, and I've never done anything bad.

"I'm doing this for your own good. You're bad, bad, bad."

I immediately take off running, away from the cemetery and away from the words that echo in my head. I make it to the water's edge in record time and stop next to an outcropping of weeds and pussy willows, calming my racing heart and pushing aside the thoughts in my head that are making me crazy.

The sun glints off of the smooth surface of the water, and I have to shield my eyes from the bright glare. With no trees in the immediate vicinity of the lake, there's nothing to shade me from the heat of the early afternoon sun, and it's not long before I feel sweat dripping down my back beneath my dress. The water looks cool and inviting and I wish I would have had the foresight to put on my bathing suit before I walked down here. Another wayward thought pops into my head as I stare out at the water: I don't own a bathing suit. Thinking about the dresses that hang in my closet and the other articles of clothing folded neatly in my dresser, I realize I haven't seen one in any of my things. I find that strange, considering we have a lake on our property with a dock attached, one that is perfect for running down and jumping into the refreshing water.

Gazing at the dock a hundred yards away, I drop my hand from shielding my eyes from the sun and make my way toward it. As I step onto the worn and rickety boards that hover over the water, excitement fills me at the thought of running across it and jumping into the water with my clothes on. I can almost feel myself sinking to the bottom of the murky water, letting it cool my sweaty skin and erase all of my bad thoughts while the darkness swallows me up and blocks out the sun. I continue walking along the dock in a daze as I survey the water, imagining my feet sinking into the mud and the sand at the bottom of the lake before pushing off and soaring back up to the surface. I want to disappear under the water and feel alive. I want to kick my feet, pull my arms through the water, and propel my body as fast as I can until I feel the burn in my muscles that makes me feel strong and in control.

I take a deep breath and hold it in my lungs, closing my eyes and lifting my foot off the end of the dock, wanting nothing more than to sink into oblivion. Spreading my arms out from my body, I feel myself falling forward and my heart speeds up in anticipation. Right when I excitedly expect to feel myself splash into the cold water, strong arms wrap around my waist, and I'm yanked backward so quickly that I shout in disappointment and anger.

"Let me go! I want to swim!" I scream, clawing at the arms around me that drag me back away from the edge of the dock.

I'm suddenly lifted up from the wood as I kick and shout in protest, the arms around me holding tighter while I longingly eye the water. The thumping of footsteps against the dock swiftly fades away as I'm moved onto the grass surrounding the lake. I continue to yell and fight against the arms that hold me, my shouts of protest immediately cut off when I'm dropped onto my butt in the grass. Ignoring the pain in my rear end from being tossed to the ground and the embarrassment of being dragged away from the water like a rag doll, I scramble up from the grass and whirl around to confront the person who put a stop to my plans.

My mouth drops open in surprise when I see Nolan standing in front of me with his hands casually resting on his hips. I should be afraid that I'm out here alone with him, far enough from the prison that no one will hear me if I scream, but I'm too angry to worry about my safety.

"What the hell are you doing?" I yell angrily.

"Saving you from drowning. A thank you would be nice," he deadpans.

Once again, I'm struck by how nice he is to look at. Just like always, he's dressed in a ratty pair of jeans and an old t-shirt that clings to his body, covered in dirt and sweat from working outside under the blazing sun. His shaggy blonde hair hangs down over one eye, making him look cute and innocent, instead of mean and imposing. I'm so furious at being taken away from the water that I forget about being afraid and mistrustful of him.

"I wasn't even *in* the water, so you didn't save me from anything," I argue, mirroring his pose by putting my own hands on my hips as I glare at him.

He shakes his head at me, rolling his eyes in annoyance.

"Oh no. You don't get to be annoyed with *me*," I continue. "You had no right to drag me away from the water. Who do you think you are, stopping me from going for a swim in *my* lake on *my* family's property?"

The irritation disappears from his face and his hands drop from his hips as he stares at me. The silence and the way he studies me is unnerving, and it makes me want to run away. Not because I'm afraid of him or what he might do to me, but because I'm scared he'll figure out all of my secrets, even the ones I can't even comprehend myself.

"Jesus," he whispers under his breath. "You really *don't* remember anything."

I hate the way he says these words, like he knows everything about me, and he's shocked that I know nothing.

"What are you talking about?"

He rubs the back of his neck nervously, finally

looking away from me to stare out at the lake behind me.

"I thought it was all an act. I thought you were ashamed of…God, I'm an asshole…"

Nolan trails off, still scanning the lake instead of looking at me. I have no idea what he's muttering about and I want to yell at him and demand answers, but the quiet confusion in his voice and the look of sadness on his face hold me back. What did he think was an act? What do I have to be ashamed of?

"You honestly don't remember. It never occurred to me you really didn't remember until I saw you on the end of that dock. Jesus, you just about took ten years off my life," he curses, letting out a frustrated breath.

"Will you please tell me what the hell you're talking about?" I ask in annoyance, fully prepared to stomp my foot if necessary.

His eyes come back to mine, and I'm overwhelmed with the grief I see shining back at me. He takes a step toward me, close enough that I can feel the heat radiating off of his body. Not even the warmth from his skin can stop the chill that skitters through me at his next words.

"Ravenna, you don't know how to swim. You're deathly afraid of the water, and you never, ever come near this lake."

I wrap my arms around my body and shake my head back and forth in denial. It doesn't make sense. I want to argue that he's wrong but I can see the truth written all over his face. He was honestly afraid for my safety. He saw me out at the end of the dock and pulled me away before I could jump in. It's impossible to be afraid of someone who clearly wanted to save me, instead of harm me. I forget about the fading bruises on my wrist that matched the fingerprints he left on my upper arm the other day because maybe he tried to save me one other time, and I just don't remember. The only things I'm afraid of right now are the things he knows about me that I don't.

Without another word, I sidestep around him and take off, fleeing toward the prison. When he shouts my name, I don't even look back. I run away from the lake, and I run away from the person who could be the key to unlocking my memories. I run because for the first time since I woke up, I'm not sure I want to know the truth.

"My name is Ravenna Duskin. I'm eighteen years old, and I live in a prison. I have dreams of swimming until my lungs want to burst...but I don't know how to swim."

CHAPTER 6

RUDELY ELBOW my way through a group of tourists milling about in the hallway, waiting their turn in the gift shop. I ignore the shouts of protests when I bump into shoulders and shove people out of my way as I run down the hallway and race up the stairs. I hear my father call my name in a worried voice, but I ignore him as well, escaping into my room and slamming the door closed behind me.

Staring at the pristine pink room with the bed neatly made, I scream in frustration, stomp over to the covers and rip them from the bed. Before I went outside this morning, I found a dark blue comforter in the bathroom closet and remade my bed with something I found appealing, instead of something that disgusted me. My mother must have switched the blankets after I left to go on my walk. In a fit of rage, I crumple the pink comforter in my arms, open the window next to my bed, and toss it out into the air. Clutching onto the windowsill, I watch it flutter to the ground, landing in a heap in the grass two stories below, and wish I could follow right along with it. Maybe a good solid fall from a second-story window will jar my brain enough that everything starts making sense.

With a frustrated growl, I turn from the window and give the metal frame of my bed a few good hard kicks. The bed shakes and rattles each time my foot connects with the frame, and after the fourth kick I hear a dull *thump* from underneath. I immediately put a halt to my temper tantrum and drop down on all fours next to the bed. Lifting the ruffled pink bedskirt with one hand, I peer beneath the bed. Lying in between a few dust bunnies and one stray sock, I see a book that must have been the cause of the noise, falling out of its hiding spot when I took my anger out on my bed. Reaching underneath the bed, I grab the book and pull it toward me, letting the ruffled skirt fall back into place as I hold the book in my hands and sit back on my feet. Skimming my hands over the worn brown leather, I realize it's a journal and excitement courses through me, even though I don't recognize the book. Obviously it's mine since it was hidden under my bed. Cradling the journal to my chest, I scoot backward to the wall directly below the window and lean against it, pulling my knees up to my chest and resting the book on top of them. Flipping open the leather cover, the first few words on the page, written in flowery, cursive script, make me smile.

"The diary of Ravenna Duskin. Keep out!"

The words *keep out* are underlined three times.

Turning over the first page, my smile fades when I'm met with a blank page. I turn to the next page and it's blank as well. Lifting the book closer to my face to inspect it better, I spread open the binding as wide as I can, my finger tracing down the center of the journal where there are several missing pages, ripped out of the book as close to the bindings as possible so as to leave barely a trace of evidence that they are gone. Shaking my head in annoyance, I quickly flip through the few remaining pages in the book, my frustration growing when I realize I won't find anything helpful, until I get to the final page in the book. My hand stills on the last page, filled with words from the very top all the way to the bottom. Every space of this page is covered with ink, including the side margins. The words at the top start out very small, almost too small to read, but as they continue down the page, they grow larger, the ink becoming darker and darker as some of the words were traced over multiple times. The pretty, flowing script on the first page doesn't look like my handwriting, even though I know it must be mine. Running my fingers over the harshly written words on this last page, I know with absolute certainty that *these* words are mine. This tight, angry block lettering is mine and these words repeated over and over again are mine. I don't recognize the journal; I don't remember ever keeping a record of my thoughts and memories, but I must have. The book was in my room, hidden beneath my bed, in a place where only I would find it. My hands shake as I skate my fingers over the words that I feel like are screaming the truth, forcing me to open my eyes and accept the reality that my mind won't allow.

The secrets are hidden in the walls of this prison.
They will destroy you before they set you free.

I slam the book closed, squeezing my eyes shut to block out the words, even though I can see them swirling around behind my eyes, angry and shouting at me to pay attention, to see what's right in front of me. My bedroom door suddenly flies open, and I quickly toss the journal under my bed and out of sight as my father races over to me, squatting down so we're at eye-level.

"Ravenna? Is everything okay?"

I focus on the concern in his voice and the worry in his eyes, instead of the words I must have written as a warning to myself before the accident. Why did I write those words repeatedly? What kinds of secrets are hidden in my home?

I look at my father in his perfectly pressed navy blue suit and his slicked-back hair and I wonder what could possibly be so horrible about the truth that someone would want to do me harm to prevent it from coming out.

"Who am I, Daddy?" I whisper brokenly, letting my head thump back against the wall.

I don't know why I'm even asking this when I

know he won't be honest with me. I've been avoiding him ever since I heard him fighting with my mother, afraid of the man who would speak so angrily to his wife and then smack her across the face when she tried to argue with him. Have I ever heard my parents fight before? I wrack my brain trying to dredge up memories from my childhood, but all I can see are those stupid family photos that adorn our living room. I can't access even *one* solid memory of the three of us together, behaving like a normal, happy family should. All I can think of is the way my parents have acted ever since I woke up, the way they avoid each other at all costs, and the way they stare at everything in the room but each other when we have dinner together. The only memory that screams in my mind so clearly is the one I recaptured when I saw the photo on our mantel. Why did that photo in particular fill me with such hatred and rage toward my parents?

I watch as my father's shoulders tense, and I try not to flinch when he reaches out and brushes a strand of hair from my eyes that must have come loose during my momentary outburst earlier. Tucking the strand behind my ear, he cups my cheek in his palm.

"You're Ravenna, my beautiful, wonderful daughter," he tells me softly. "The same person you've always been."

"Just keep reminding her who she is and everything

will be fine."

The words my father spoke to my mother play on a loop in my mind, and I can feel my temper begin to flare. My hands clench into fists in my lap and I feel my fingernails digging roughly into my palms.

"I know it's frustrating, but the doctor said it would take time," he reminds me with a placating smile. "Just stop trying to force things, or you'll make it worse."

I've heard these same words so many times in the last few days that I want to smack his hand away and scream in his face. I want to grab the lapels of his suit jacket and shake him until he stops feeding me the same bullshit and is honest with me. How could things possibly get any worse? Every time I close my eyes, I'm afraid a new memory will pop up, leaving me scared and even more confused, and now I have a journal that I don't even remember owning, let alone writing in, missing all of its pages except for the one with a scary, cryptic message in it. Is there *really* something worse than this reality?

"Do I know how to swim?"

He looks startled by my question but hides his surprise with a chuckle, dropping his hands from the side of my face.

"Goodness, no! We could barely get you to take a bath when you were little."

He closes his eyes for a moment, and his face looks peaceful as he most likely reminisces about my childhood.

"Why was I so afraid of the water?" I ask softly.

He opens his eyes and sighs, waving his hand in the air as if he's brushing off the question.

"Just a little accident that happened when you were little. It really wasn't that big of a deal," he answers, giving me a tight smile as he rests his arms on his knees. "These silly questions aren't going to help. All you need to do is get back to your normal schedule, spend your days just like you always did, and things will fall into place."

It enrages me that he thinks my questions are silly. Why is figuring out the parts of my memory that I'm missing considered silly? Why is trying to understand who I am a waste of time?

"Why can't you just be honest with me?" I whisper desperately.

He pushes against his knees with his palms to stand up. Sliding his hands into the front pockets of his suit pants, he jangles the loose change in there and stares down at me.

"I don't know what you expect me to say, Ravenna. Why would you think I'm not being honest with you?" he asks me with a frustrated sigh.

"Why was I in the woods that night?" I immediately fire back, refusing to back down.

He squares his shoulders and lifts his chin. "Your mother and I have already told you we don't know."

"Fine, you don't know why I was out in the

woods in the middle of the night during a thunder-storm," I reply sarcastically. "Then who found me? How did you even know I was hurt and to call the doctor?"

It never occurred to me to ask this question until now. The only wooded area on our property is on the other side of the lake, more than an acre away. If that's where I got hurt, how would anyone have even known to look for me out there, unless they saw me leave the house? Unless they were following me.

Unless they were chasing me.

I can see myself running as fast as I can through the dark woods, tripping over tree roots and stray branches. I can almost feel my heart pounding in my chest as I run away from something, but it's not because of fear. I'm proud of something I've done, and I'm angry that I'm being forced to run away from it instead of confront it.

My father sighs in frustration, the sound pulling me out of my thoughts. "I can't answer your questions, Ravenna. I was busy working in my office, and I heard your mother scream. I ran downstairs and saw you unconscious on the floor, and I immediately called the doctor."

It doesn't escape my notice that he told me he *can't* answer my questions, not that he didn't know the answers to them.

Unfortunately, even his partial answers are the same my mother gave me, and they don't help me at all. She was getting out of the shower and heard a noise downstairs. She came down and saw me lying in the middle of the floor, sopping wet, covered in dirt and leaves, with scratches all over my arms and a head wound that wouldn't stop bleeding.

"Why does everything I remember feel like it's the exact opposite of what you and Mom tell me?" I question.

He immediately stops playing with the spare change in his pocket and silence fills the room. I hate that I'm sitting on the floor at his feet, feeling so small and insignificant when he towers over me so commanding and in charge, ignoring everything I ask him as if the questions I have aren't worthy of an answer. I want to stand up to him, yell in his face, and poke his chest with my finger, but I find myself glued to the floor as the mask of indifference on his face quickly changes to one of fear. His eyes widen and he bites down nervously on his bottom lip, much like my mother did when I walked in her room and caught her crying.

"Have you remembered something, Ravenna? What have you remembered?" he asks in a rush.

His concern would be touching if I felt like he was doing it for my benefit, instead of trying to figure out if I've remembered something I shouldn't. Something that would prove he really has been lying to me and he knows what happened.

Because he saw it happen, or because he was the

cause of it?

Once again, I'm left wondering what could possibly be so bad that my own father doesn't want me to know the truth.

Maybe I haven't been avoiding him lately because I'm afraid of him and uncomfortable around him ever since I heard him yelling at my mother. Maybe I've been avoiding him because I'm afraid of how he makes me feel in his presence. When I'm in the same room with him, I feel my mistrust of him growing so strongly that it's almost suffocating. A daughter should trust her father and know without a shadow of a doubt that everything he does is to protect her, but when I look at him, sometimes I feel nothing but anger and disappointment. I feel as if this isn't the first time he's ever let me down.

Right now, if someone were to ask, I could recite a laundry list of things my father has done to prove his love for me over the years, but that's all it would be...a list. I don't have the memories that should go along with those things. I don't remember sitting on his knee while he read me a story, I don't remember him holding my hair back while I blew out birthday candles on a cake, and I don't remember splashing around in puddles in the driveway. I've seen the photos in the albums and hanging on the walls, but I *can't remember them.* I should be able to remember the smell of the smoke from freshly blown-out candles; I should remember the soft sound of his melodic voice as he read to me, and I should be able to feel the mud and the water splashing against my legs in the driveway. Why do I *know* things but I can't *feel* them?

"Ravenna!"

He calls my name again, obviously impatient that I haven't answered his question. He wants to know if I've remembered anything. If I really were the good girl, the perfect daughter, the *wonderful* daughter they keep telling me I am, maybe I'd do as I'm told and stop forcing things and asking questions. Maybe I'd push aside all of my crazy thoughts and strange glimpses into memories that confuse me and just go about my life, content to believe whatever they tell me and not worry about things I can't remember. Maybe I'd learn to love the color pink and stop getting headaches every time my mother braids my hair too tight.

"The secrets are hidden in the walls of this prison," I tell him in a monotone voice, repeating the words that were written in my journal.

I watch as the color drains from his face and instead of being horrified with myself for finding pleasure in his fear, I let it travel through me, igniting me and making me feel alive for the first time in days.

My father slowly backs away from me, his eyes never leaving my face.

"I'll just let you get some rest. I need to get back to the tour," he informs me as he bumps into the wall next to my bedroom door.

He gives me a tight smile before he turns and

leaves my room, closing the door behind him.

"My name is Ravenna Duskin. I'm eighteen years old, I live in a prison, and I'm pretty sure I'm not a good girl."

CHAPTER 7

AFTER MY FATHER left my room, I tore the place apart, looking for the pages of the journal that had been ripped out. I don't know why those pages are missing, and I don't like it. Finding nothing hidden in any nook or cranny anywhere in my room, I searched the only other room upstairs that wasn't locked or occupied—the kitchen—and found nothing. My father had been working in his office and my mother was holed up in her room so those two areas would have to wait until they left and the spare bedroom would have to wait for me to either pick the lock or find the key in my father's office. Making a quick sandwich in the kitchen since I had no desire to sit through another silent, awkward dinner with my parents, I ate outside on the front porch and enjoyed the peace and quiet with nothing but the sounds of birds chirping and frogs croaking.

My eyes searched the grounds in front of the prison, hoping for a glimpse of Nolan. It seems weird to be seeking out the person I'd spent the last few days being afraid of, but at this point he might be the only person here I can trust. It's impossible to fear someone who went out of his way to save my life. If he was the one who hurt me or wanted to do me more harm, he could have easily just let me jump in the lake. Or he could have pushed me. I was so busy imagining the feel of the cool water on my skin that I never even heard him come up behind me.

Not finding him anywhere in my sight line, it occurs to me that I don't hear the sound of the lawn mowers in the distance or men's voices chatting as they work and I realize everyone must have gone home for the day. He always seems to be watching me and waiting for me any other time I've gone outside and, of course, now that I actually want to talk to him, he's nowhere to be found.

As I continue eating, I flip open the photo album I brought outside and placed on the porch next to me. Under a few of the photos from my childhood, there is a small white strip of tape with my mother's pretty cursive script, explaining what certain photos are.

Ravenna's tenth birthday!

Ravenna learning to ride a bike!

Christmas morning with Ravenna!

Each photo I look at fills me with unnatural anger at the happy, smiling child I see on the pages, and I don't know why. Shouldn't I be happy seeing proof of how normal and wonderful my childhood was? Instead, I want to rip each photo from its clear plastic sheet, tear them all into a thousand pieces and scream that it was all a lie. I hate the child in the photos. I hate that her life looks so perfect in black and white when the reality of living color is the exact opposite.

On the last page, I see one photo by itself in the middle: a picture of both my parents fishing in the lake, and looking toward the camera with smiles on their faces. Off to the very edge of the photo, at least a hundred feet from my parents, staring at the water with wide, frightened eyes is ten-year-old me. Under the picture my mother has written: *A day of fishing! Poor Ravenna won't go near the water, as usual.*

With a heavy sigh, I slam the album closed and toss my half-eaten sandwich on the plate, my appetite suddenly gone. Scooping up the album and my dish, I head upstairs to put the dirty dish in the kitchen sink, and then wander into my bedroom, tossing the album onto my bed.

I stare at the mess I made of my room and decide to leave it for now as I flop down on the bed on my back, staring up at the ceiling. An idea pops into my head and I quickly roll onto my stomach and lean over the edge of my bed, reaching underneath for the journal I quickly tossed there when my father came in. I'm tired of feeling that, at any moment, the things I've remembered are going to slip right from my grasp. Even if the journal is missing a bunch of pages that could possibly give me answers, there are still a few blank ones left where I could write things down that I've already figured out. Like how I hate pink, hate having my hair braided, hate all my clothes, and I don't know how to swim. How quickly I get angry when something makes me mad, even though I'm supposedly sweet and good, and how I have memories of feeling so much pain that it takes my breath away. So many things that don't add up, but maybe if I write them down and look at them long enough it will all come together.

Feeling around blindly with my hands, I come up empty. Scooting my body more over the edge, I lift up the bedskirt and stare underneath my bed at nothing but an empty floor. Someone took my journal. I was only out of my room long enough to search the kitchen and eat a quick dinner. As far as I know, the only two people here right now are my parents, since the handful of tour guides, the receptionist, and the grounds crew have all gone home for the evening. My parents are the only ones who could have taken it, but why? It's not like there was anything useful in it, since half of the pages were missing. *I* didn't even remember that I'd kept a journal, so how would *they* know of its existence and where it was located?

When I hear the click of heels moving across the living room floor in the direction of my room, I groan and quickly push myself up on the bed, curling my legs under me and wait for my mother to barge in. I'm sure my father has told her all about how I behaved earlier, and she's most likely going to give me hell for the way I acted with him. As the minutes ticked by after my father left my room, I replayed what happened over and over in my head while I searched for the journal pages. Even *I* realized my behavior was strange, no matter how good it felt, no matter how *right* it felt. I probably should have gone to him and apologized. I'm sure the "old me" would have done it, but I couldn't apologize for something I wasn't sorry about. I'm so tired of faking everything and trying to be the girl I just don't know how to be. Nothing feels right about any of it. I'm supposed to be good and polite and not ask questions when everything in my head is telling me to be bad and loud and question everything.

My door swings open and I lift my chin, filling myself with confidence for the scolding I'm sure to get. She can go right ahead and yell at me, and when she's through, I'll ask her what the hell she did with my journal.

My mother takes one look around my room at the mess I've made, tossing clothing out of every drawer of my dresser and chucking shoes and other miscellaneous items out of my closet, and huffs in annoyance.

"What on earth happened to your room, Ravenna?" she asks, as she bends down and picks up a pile of socks and underwear right next to the door, walking over to one of my open dresser drawers and depositing everything inside.

I watch in silence as she continues picking things up and putting them away.

"Honestly, Ravenna, I know things are difficult right now, but that doesn't mean you can just behave any way you like," she complains as she hangs up a pale purple dress in my closet.

When she has most of the items picked up from my floor, she comes over to my bed and sits down on the edge of it, folding her hands in her lap as she stares into my eyes. It makes me just as uncomfortable as it always does, but I refuse to look away. I refuse to cower when she tells me the way I spoke to my father was inexcusable. What's inexcusable is my being made to feel guilty because I want to know what happened to me, and my mother taking something out of my room that belongs to me.

"We need to talk about something very serious."

Here it comes…

My mother takes a deep breath before reaching over and grabbing my hands, giving them a squeeze.

"Why in the world is your beautiful pink bedding out on the lawn below your window?"

She looks at me so solemnly that I can't stop the laugh that bursts out of me. Her eyes narrow in annoyance, and it just makes me laugh harder.

"This is not funny, Ravenna," she scolds. "Do you have any idea how expensive that bedding was? And you just toss it out onto the grass as if it's nothing."

Leave it to my mother to think *this* is an issue of importance right now.

"I hate those blankets. The color is disgusting,

and I don't want them on my bed," I tell her.

"You always loved the color pink," she whispers sadly.

Pulling my hands out of hers, I cross them in front of me. "Well, I don't like it now. I think it's pretty clear some things have changed around here lately."

She bites her bottom lip nervously and finally looks away from me to stare out the window next to my bed.

"Everything is going to be fine, you'll see," she speaks softly.

I'm not sure if her words are for me, or if she's trying to convince herself.

"Nothing will be *fine* until I get answers, until I can remember all of the things that no one seems to care about helping me figure out," I tell her angrily. "Until someone tells me why my journal is missing from my room."

She turns her head back to look at me, tilting it to the side. She reaches her hand out toward me, but I back out of her reach. I don't want her comfort. I want answers.

"Journal? What journal?" she asks, trying to hide the hurt she felt when I pulled away from her. "Ravenna, I don't know what this is all about, but of course we want to help you. I would give anything to fix things, but I don't know how."

I let the journal problem go for the time being

since she really does seem clueless about it. Instead, I focus on the fact that maybe she's telling the truth. Maybe she really would do anything to make things better.

"You can fix it by telling me the truth. Just tell me the truth, for God's sake!" I shout, unable to keep my anger and frustration in check no matter how kind and loving she is with me.

"I would never lie to you."

I scoff and shake my head at her. "Of course you would, just like Dad told you to do. Just keep reminding me who I am, and everything will be fine, right? Just keep doing what he says, even if you know something isn't right, that something is wrong with me. Don't worry about having a mind of your own; just keep following along like the obedient little sheep you are."

The smack across my cheek comes quickly and without warning, although I should have expected it. What I don't expect is the flash of memory that bursts through my mind as soon as I feel the sting of her palm against the side of my face.

"You disrespectful little bitch! How dare you speak to me that way!"

Pressing my hand to my cheek to ease the sting, I glare at her as the anger on her face quickly fades and is replaced by regret.

"Oh my God. Oh Ravenna, I'm so sorry. I've never done anything like that before. I'm so sorry," she pleads as tears pool in her eyes.

Lies.

She stood in front of me once before, in the spare bedroom with the dark blue quilt I prefer and pale blue walls, her face red with fury as she smacked me across the face and called me names. The thunder boomed outside and the rain beat against the window as she stormed out of the room and told me I wasn't allowed to come out as she slammed the door behind her.

Even with the depressing way she always looks at me and the way she keeps trying to make me into someone I'm clearly not with the braiding of my hair and the pink bedspread, I still had a small glimmer of hope she would be honest with me and stand up for me after the argument I heard her having with my father. Those hopes flew out the window like that stupid, ugly blanket as soon as she smacked me and lied about never doing anything like that before.

"Get. Out."

I watch the tears fall down her cheeks, and I don't even care that I've made her cry.

"Ravenna, please," she begs through her tears. "I'm so sorry. I never—"

"GET OUT!" I scream, cutting her off as I point to my door.

She quickly jumps up from my bed and much like my father earlier in the day, backs out of the room with a look of fear on her face.

Good. They *should* fear me. If they aren't going to help me, they damn well better be afraid of the day I finally figure everything out. The only thing that shocks me about the exchange with my mother is that she never mentioned what happened with my father. There's no way she would have just swept that under the rug. It would have been the perfect opportunity for her to remind me how good and sweet I'm supposed to be. As husband and wife, two people who supposedly love each other, shouldn't my father have told her what I said? Shouldn't he have been concerned enough about my odd statement about secrets being hidden that he went to her for help, so they could tackle the problem as a team? Not only are they keeping things from me, they're keeping things from each other.

"My name is Ravenna Duskin. I'm eighteen years old, I live in a prison, and I will find out the truth, even if it destroys everyone around me."

CHAPTER 8

"B UT, SIR. WE came all the way out here today just to fill in that hole," Ike complains.

"I said go home and tell the rest of the men their services won't be needed tonight either," my father replies firmly.

Keeping my back pressed to the wall right outside the door leading down to the basement, I stay as still as possible, so no one knows I'm there as the two men argue on the stairs below. I came out of my hiding place when I heard voices, and I know I should have stayed where I was, but I had to know what was going on. I had to know what my father would do to try and fix the problem that he created. Now that I know, it makes me want to laugh. For the last few weeks I've seen him ripping into Ike almost every day about filling the hole in the basement and how it should have been done by now. It's quite hilarious that all of a sudden he's changed his mind, and now he looks like a fool.

You won't be able to hide your secrets forever, Daddy dearest.

"I don't understand, Mr. Duskin. You've been asking us to fill in the hole in the sub-basement for months. I've been making calls for weeks to get an order of fill-dirt in and I had to call in a lot of favors to have it delivered on a Sunday," Ike explains.

"How many times do I have to tell you?!" my father bellows, his voice bouncing off of the stone walls in the small stairwell. "I've changed my mind. The hole stays."

"But, sir—"

"GET OUT THIS INSTANT IF YOU WANT TO CONTINUE WORKING HERE!" my father interrupts, his voice rising above the storm that rages outside. "Your stupidity and carelessness has already done enough damage. Figure out a way to fix this mess instead of making things worse."

I hear a few mumbled curses and the shuffling of feet on the stairs, one set moving farther down them into the basement and the other coming up closer to me. I move as quickly and quietly as possible across the hall to the artifact museum, but I'm not fast enough.

"What are you running from, little girl?" Ike asks.

I slowly turn in the doorway of the museum and watch him close the basement door behind him, before walking down the hallway toward me. He's a tall man in his mid-forties, well over six feet, and his arms are the size of tree stumps. He's wearing dark blue coveralls and a t-shirt that probably used to be white at one time, but is so saturated with dirt and sweat that it looks grey. He's been a groundskeeper here for over ten years and my father recently started letting him do a tour every once in a while when we're busy. He thinks that makes him special. He thinks that makes him an authority on everything that happens here, but he doesn't know everything. He doesn't know what I'm capable of. He's been watching me for weeks, sticking his nose in my business, no matter where I am or what I'm doing, and I've had enough.

He continues moving down the hall until he's toe-to-toe with me, and I stand my ground, refusing to move or let him intimidate me even when the smell of his sweat makes me gag. Ike leans down until his mouth is right next to my ear.

"You might be able to fool everyone else, girly, but I know what you did. I know what you are."

I grit my teeth when he pulls back and laughs, his hot breath reeking of onions as it puffs across my face.

"What I am is someone you should stay far, far away from," I tell him with a smile, cutting off his mocking laughter.

The confidence on his face vanishes, and I smile even wider when I watch his Adam's apple bob as he swallows nervously.

The pounding of footsteps up the basement stairs is the only thing that could make me move from where I'm standing. I might not fear the disgusting man standing in front of me, or the one stomping up the stairs, but that doesn't mean I'm an idiot. With a glance around Ike's giant body, I turn and run around the stairs toward the front door.

I hear Ike laugh behind me as I quickly yank the heavy door open.

"Run away, little girl, run away! There's nowhere you can hide now!" Ike shouts, his laughter back as I race *down the steps and out into the pouring rain.*

My eyes open slowly and I sit up, rubbing the sleep out of them. For the first time in the last few days, I actually remember my entire dream, instead of bits and pieces that don't make any sense. I don't wake up covered in sweat, fearing the things I dreamed that I couldn't remember. I still don't understand what my memories are trying to tell me, but at least I have another piece of the puzzle to add to my growing pile of mismatched pieces.

Flinging the blankets off of me, I pause as I stare down at the dark blue comforter my mother must have put on my bed when I was in the bathroom, cleaning up for bed. I'm sure it was her way of making amends for what happened, but it didn't work. Acknowledging my hatred of a stupid color of a blanket doesn't make up for the knowledge that I officially cannot trust either one of my parents.

Jumping out of bed, I pull open my bottom dresser drawer and yank out the one pair of jeans I own that I found in the back of my closet yesterday when I tore my room apart. Grabbing the pair of scissors sitting in a plastic cup on top of the dresser, I quickly shear off the stiff material from the upper thigh down. I pull the newly cut jean shorts up my legs and under my nightgown, immediately loving the way they feel. With the scissors still in my hand, I take them to the waist of my tank top gown, cutting an uneven line around my body until the bottom lacy half of it flutters to the floor at my feet. Slamming the scissors down on the dresser, I pull the rubber band out of the end of my hair and roughly scrub my hands through my scalp, untangling the braid my mother put in yesterday morning.

When I'm finished, I look at myself in the mirror and finally smile at the reflection staring back at me. The top of the nightgown that is now a tank top is made of flimsy cotton material and if you look hard enough, you can clearly see my breasts through it. The now tiny jean shorts make my bare legs look a mile long, and my thick black hair hanging in loose waves down my back makes me look wild and older than my eighteen years. Turning away from my reflection, I pad softly across my hardwood floor, quietly open my door, and listen for any sounds of my parents. As much as I want to continue pestering and arguing with them until one of them finally breaks and admits something truthful to me, I'm more concerned about my dream and figuring out all of the events surrounding what happened that night.

When I hear nothing but silence upstairs, I move through the living room and down to the first floor. At the bottom, I walk around the banister and head in the opposite direction of the front door. When I get to the back of the stairs, I walk to the door hidden against the wall underneath them. Glancing quickly around me to make sure I'm alone, I take a few seconds to stand here quietly and listen for the sounds of someone approaching. When I hear nothing but the ticking of the old grandfather clock at the opposite end of the hall in the artifact museum, I move forward and stare at the door that leads to the basement—the first stop on the tour of the prison. It's the one that equally excites and scares people at the same time. Basements in old buildings are always scary, but a basement in an old prison where solitary confinement was located and lots of unspeakable acts were inflicted upon prisoners, some fatally, is chilling.

I know the basement is mostly empty, and the temperature drops a few degrees as soon as one gets to the bottom of the steps. It's pretty common for that to happen in a room located underground, but there's something different about the air down there. It's even colder than it should be and every once in a while, visitors walk through an extra frigid pocket of air that can never be explained since the basement has no windows. I feel like some part of me has never liked the basement just like that same part of me supposedly never liked going into the cell blocks, like my father said. Then there's the other part, the one screaming to get out, the one who feels freer with her hair down and out of a stuffy dress, who wants to go down there, who feels something pulling her in that direction, just like in the cell block.

My father lost his temper when the men came to work in the basement. I remember so clearly the need to laugh at how resolute he was that no one goes down in the basement. There's got to be a reason why I dreamt about hearing that conversation. There's got to be a reason why I itch with excitement to open this door and go down those stairs, why my body practically hums with eager energy, knowing that what lies beyond this door could be the answer to all the secrets I can't figure out and that no one wants to tell me. Having that dream reminded me of the several times I heard my father arguing with Ike and a few of the other men about the hole in the basement. It's located in a separate room at the far end and while it gives the tours an additional creepy factor when visitors hear about what happened down in that hole in the 1800's, it's also a danger. Located directly over a natural spring, every time it rains the hole fills with water, and my father was growing concerned that keeping it intact was too much of a liability. Why, all of a sudden, was he so adamant that no one goes down there? Why, after weeks and months of complaining about having it filled in, did he suddenly change his mind?

Wrapping my hand around the knob, I quickly turn it and I'm immediately met with resistance. I rattle the knob harder, pulling on the door at the same time, but it doesn't open. It's locked. The only doors ever locked in the prison on tour days are the ones upstairs in our living quarters, in case visitors happen to wander where they aren't supposed to go.

Checking the watch on my wrist, I see that the

prison has been open for business for over an hour. Even on days when we don't have tours booked, people are welcome to come in and check out the gift shop and museum and as long as there aren't any internal repairs going on, my father will usually allow them to wander through certain areas on their own if they don't want a guide to explain things to them. No part of the prison should be locked up right now. The fact that the one area I need to explore is closed up tight ticks me off and I slam my palm against the wood, muttering a few colorful curses under my breath.

"I didn't realize good girls knew that kind of language."

I whirl around to find Nolan leaning against the banister of the stairs with a smile on his face.

"Well, luckily I'm not a good girl," I growl, rolling my eyes as I stomp past him.

He jogs to catch up, racing around me to block me from going out the front door.

"What's got you in a bad mood?" he asks as I shuffle to the side to get around him, but he easily moves with me, continuing to hinder my escape from this frustrating place.

"People who lie to me tend to piss me off. Now get out of my way."

I shove him roughly aside and even though he's got a good sixty pounds on me and could have held his ground, he moves to let me pass. Unfortunately, he follows me right outside. My bare feet slap against the wood as I stomp down the steps and make a left, heading to the lake.

"You want to talk about it?" he asks from behind me.

Realizing he's just going to keep following me, and I did just decide yesterday that I wanted to talk to him, I stop in the middle of the yard under the shade of a large oak tree and turn to face him.

"Fine, you want to talk? Let's talk. Tell me how you knew I didn't know how to swim," I fire at him.

With my head held high, I try not to think about how dumb I sounded the other day when I had no clue I didn't know how to swim and the way I freaked out and ran away without saying another word to him. I am not going to let him make me feel silly just because he knows things about me that I don't re-member. I'm going to use it to my advantage and hope that he's more honest with me than my parents.

"Wow, getting right to the point, I see," he says with a smile as he slides his hands into the back pock-et of his jeans.

I tap my foot against the ground and raise my eyebrow, waiting for him to answer my question. He sighs and leans his shoulder casually against the side of the tree.

"I've worked here for two years," he replies.

"I already knew that. It doesn't answer my ques-tion. How did you know I couldn't swim?"

He doesn't look away from me and even though it makes me uncomfortable to be stared at so openly, it also makes me feel like he won't lie to me. People seem to look away from me when they tell me things I find difficult to believe.

"There aren't that many of us who work here at the prison," he begins. "We're a pretty tight group since we work with each other all day, every day, and a couple of the guys have been here a lot longer than me. People hear things, people talk. Most of it is stupid bullshit gossip. Someone mentioned one time how weird it was that you were so afraid of the water and how you'd never go anywhere near the lake.

He shrugs easily, like it's no big deal the people who work here talk about me behind my back.

"So you knew from workplace gossip?" I scoff.

"Initially, yes. But I asked you a few weeks ago if it was true and you told me so yourself. Something about an accident when you were little. Five, I think. You didn't tell me much, just that you've been petrified of water ever since."

My arms drop to my sides while I mull this over. Something seems familiar about what he's telling me. I don't know if it's because some part of me remembers it, or because I remember telling him. I just know, deep down inside, that there was something that happened in water when I was little. I don't know why it feels right, it just does. It also leaves me with more questions. Why can I see myself swimming? Why, when I close my eyes, can I almost feel the water sluicing against my skin, feel my muscles burn as I do laps, know exactly what it feels like to pull my arms through the water and exactly what it looks like to open my eyes when I'm under there? How do I just instinctively know what all of this feels like and looks like if I it's not true? It's the same kind of thing with my stupid braided hair and all of the ugly dresses in my closet. I just *know* when it's not right, when it feels alien.

"Why did you look at me like you hated me that day you dropped off flowers for my father?" I ask next. Clearly if I we had personal conversations before the accident, he must not have hated me that much.

He looks away from me, but I see his cheeks redden and I know it's from embarrassment and not because he's crafting a lie.

"What do you want me to tell you, Ravenna?" he whispers as he stares down at his feet and kicks a stray rock away with the toe of his work boot.

"I want you to tell me the truth!" I shout at him, throwing my hands up in exasperation. "My parents have done nothing but lie to me these last few days and I'm sick and tired of it. I guess I just assumed that you were different. I figured that someone who would save a girl from drowning herself might actually be a good guy."

He runs a hand nervously through his hair and puffs out a huge breath of air through his lips. I'm immediately hit with a memory of kissing him. It was dark outside and we were on the front porch. There was lightning off in the distance and the night was hot and muggy. His lips were soft and like nothing I'd ever felt before. I remember doing it because I knew it was wrong and that excited me. I was angry. *So angry.* Filled with so much hatred that I wasn't sure if I wanted to hit him or kiss him. I went with the kiss and instead of it making me feel better, it only made me madder because I liked it so much. I didn't want to like it. I did it to prove a point and it all backfired. I remember slamming the door in his face, laughing at the shock on it.

"Jesus," he mutters, interrupting my thoughts and pulling my eyes away from his lips. "Okay, fine. You want to know the truth? The truth is, I've had kind of a thing for you for two years and you've never given me the time of day that entire time. That is, up until two weeks ago. All of a sudden, you started seeking me out when I was working. I should have known something was off, but I was too damn happy that you were finally talking to me. You were so different from the girl I'd been watching from afar for two years. Different from the rumors I'd heard and the things I'd seen with my own eyes."

"Different how?" I whisper, unsure if I want him to answer since I'm starting to realize that I might have been a really awful person before all of this happened.

"I don't know, just different. Your hair was always perfectly done and your dresses were always perfectly pressed. You walked around with your nose up in the air like you were better than everyone," he informs me.

"Well, that explains why you had a crush on me. I sound like a wonderful person," I reply sarcastically.

"Ravenna, I'm a guy. And you are very, very beautiful. My crush was only skin deep, believe me."

That makes me feel so much better.

"Until two weeks ago," he continues. "Then you were just…completely different than what I thought. You wore your hair down whenever you came to see me and you always had on jeans and a t-shirt, like right now. For the first time, I didn't feel like I was a complete loser not worthy of your time. It was definitely weird that you started doing this out of the blue, but I wasn't about to question it. I liked spending time with you. I guess I was pissed that day I dropped off the flowers because, all of a sudden, you were back to being the snobby girl with the perfect hair and the perfect clothes. And you clearly wanted nothing to do with me all over again."

I can't even be happy about the *beautiful* comment or that he liked spending time with me. I'm too busy being stuck on the fact that I was a huge snob. I was mean *and* I was a snob.

"And so you just naturally assumed I was faking a brain injury so I wouldn't have to own up to treating you like a human being for the first time in two years," I reply sarcastically. "That's just wonderful."

He takes a step toward me and he's so close that I have to crane my neck to look up at him. His eyes are the most gorgeous shade of blue I've ever seen and I have a hard time looking away from them. I feel like I've waited my whole life for someone to look at me like I mean something to them and it makes my stomach churn and fills me with anger that I never got what I deserved. I deserved a good life, I deserved to be loved, and it's not fair that the only thing I ever got was pain.

That thought...those words ringing in my head are so familiar that it makes my chest ache. I know those thoughts are true and something I believe with all of my heart. Something I cried and screamed and raged about for so long that it became my mantra, my way of life, and something I knew I would spend the rest of my life feeling because there would never be any escape from the pain.

I take a step away from Nolan and close my eyes, trying to picture myself saying these things. Trying to envision my surroundings and what would make me feel so desolate, but all I see is the darkness behind my eyelids.

"If it makes you feel any better, I definitely prefer the way you look right now," Nolan says softly as I reopen my eyes to look at him.

"And how is that?" I whisper.

He shrugs, sliding his hands back into his pockets. "You look like *you*. Not like you're trying to be someone else."

It's the most perfect thing he could have said to me right now and it gives me hope that I'm not crazy for feeling *off* whenever I look in the mirror. Since Nolan seems to have no problem being honest with me even if what he has to say brings him some embarrassment, I move on to one last question.

"How well do you know Ike Jenson?"

Nolan flinches at the mention of Ike's name.

"He's been here since I started, keeps to himself a lot. Why?" Nolan asks, one of his hands coming up to rub the back of his neck in a nervous gesture.

"My father mentioned something about how he hasn't been to work in a few days and I wondered if that was typical for him."

His eyes narrow and he cocks his head to the side while he thinks about what I've said. "You know, now that you mention it, he hasn't been here since the day you got hurt. I've been so busy around here that I didn't even think about it until you said something."

I don't believe in coincidences. Especially after remembering the conversation I overheard with Ike and my father that night. I start walking away from Nolan, my mind already moving in hyper-speed as I plan what to do next.

Nolan grabs onto my hips to stop me, turning my body back around to face him. For just one moment I wish I could be a normal teenager and appreciate the man holding onto me, flirt with him, and enjoy the moment. Unfortunately, I'm not a normal girl, and I'm pretty sure I never will be.

"If he comes back, stay away from him, Ravenna. That guy is bad news," Nolan warns.

I laugh as I step away from him once more, missing the comfort of his hands on my body as soon as they fall away.

"Funny, that's exactly what my father said about *you*."

I walk away from him without another word and he lets me go this time. As I make my way back to the prison alone, I step through the doors feeling a little better than I did when I ran out of them earlier.

"My name is Ravenna Duskin. I'm eighteen years old, I live in a prison, and I'm finished being the girl my parents want me to be."

CHAPTER 9

S TOP FIGHTING, STOP *splashing, just go under and let go.*

The water churns angrily with each uncoordinated swipe of an arm, trying to reach for something to help, something to grab ahold of, but it's no use. There's nothing that will help, nothing that will save you.

Just go under. It will all be over soon if you just go under.

The cold water covers chin, mouth, nose, wide, frightened eyes and then…gone.

That's it, disappear, go away, everyone will be happier if you just go away. Don't listen to the screams and the shouts because they won't get here in time. They won't be able to take the pain away; they've NEVER been able to take the pain away. It will be so much better if you don't exist.

Swallow the water, breathe it in, close your eyes and just slip away. It will only hurt for a moment, and then you'll be free.

Don't you want to be free from the pain? Free from the evil that lurks inside your head and follows you everywhere you go?

They don't want to save me; they just want me to

disappear.

I'll show them what it's like to lose it all; I'll make them regret it.

Let yourself sink to the bottom, let them see what happens when they close their eyes and ignore the pain they caused.

Breathe it in, swallow the water, let your lungs fill until they burst, and show them.

Show them what happens when you try to hide secrets.

Show them that death is the only way to escape the pain of what they've done.

They brought this on themselves. Their hope, their future, their secrets...sinking to the bottom of the lake, dying right in front of their eyes...

Stop fighting.

Just let go.

It will all be over soon.

With a loud gasp, my eyes fly open, and I stumble backward, my head whipping around frantically as I stare at my surroundings. Digging the heels of my palms into my eyes, I rub the sleep from them before looking around once more. There's nothing but darkness around me, aside from the bright full moon reflecting off the surface of the lake.

Why am I at the lake in the middle of the night?

Staring down the front of my body, I see that I'm still wearing the pink cotton nightgown I put on before bed. My bare feet stand on the rickety wood at the end of the dock and they're wet, covered in dew and damp blades of grass from walking across the property to get here, and I realize I must have been sleepwalking. The humidity in the air covers my skin in a thin sheen of sweat and as I stare out at the moonlit lake, the cool water calls to me. The quiet peacefulness of the night, filled only with the sounds of chirping crickets and croaking bullfrogs, distracts me from the scary thought that I wandered down here alone in the middle of the night while I slept.

What if I'd fallen in? What if I'd *jumped* in? I'm out here alone, in the middle of the night, and my parents would never know I was down here because they assume I'm asleep in my bed, safe and tucked in where I'm supposed to be. They wouldn't hear me scream from this far away and they wouldn't be able to save me. I think about my dream, a memory of the accident I've been told about that happened when I was little and the cause for me being afraid of water and never learning how to swim. My heated body suddenly gets a chill and I wrap my arms around myself. Maybe they were right. Maybe they didn't lie to me about this one thing. Looking out at the dark water, I can see myself sinking under, my eyes wide with panic as the water covers my mouth and my nose, but I don't feel afraid. In my dream it felt like I was outside of my body, looking down at myself, urging that little girl to let the water take her. I feel excitement coursing through me as I picture that day and see myself disappear beneath the water. Happiness overwhelms me knowing it will all be over soon and the pain will finally stop.

I stare out at the rippling water as fish move beneath the surface. The light from the moon slowly begins to disappear as a cloud moves in front of it. I'm still groggy from sleep and on edge knowing I walked down here alone in the middle of the night without remembering doing it, but I still have an unnatural urge to jump into the water. I want to know without a shadow of a doubt which of my memories is real. I immediately shake the thought from my mind. Even half asleep, I'm still not stupid enough to do something so foolish. I will not put my life at risk just to test out a theory to prove I'm right, no matter how much I want to.

Lifting my foot to take a step back from the edge of the dock, something hard suddenly slams into my back with enough force to make me lose my balance. I don't have time to scream; I don't have time to turn my head. I can do nothing but windmill my arms through the air as I pitch forward into nothingness. I gasp in fear and shock when my body hits the cool water, swallowing a mouthful as I go under. I'm immediately swallowed by darkness as I sink to the bottom like a rock. I open my mouth to scream and more water flows inside, into my lungs and up my nose. I forget everything but the dream and the need to let go and allow the darkness to take me. I forget to fight; I forget to move my arms and legs, and I forget the pain. There's no pain down here at the bottom of the lake. There's no confusion, no lying, no secrets…nothing but silence and freedom from everything that hurts.

"Bad girls get what they deserve. It's time for you to let go and accept what you are. There's no saving you, and there never will be."

I don't want this. I don't deserve this. I can't let it end this way—it's not fair. I've always been a fighter and I won't let them win. I *can't* let them win. My lungs are on fire and my body feels numb, but I refuse to give up. I force my mind back into focus and concentrate, letting my adrenaline and instinct kick in. I start scissoring my legs and pushing my arms through the water. As my body slowly begins to lift from the bottom of the lake, determination flows through me, as I access an ability that I now know I have. My arms glide through the water with efficient, perfectly executed breaststrokes as my legs kick harder and faster behind me, propelling me upwards so fast that my head breaks the surface within seconds. I cough and spit out the water from my lungs, my legs in constant motion to keep my head above water.

Pain radiates from the middle of my back as I continue moving my limbs, reminding me that I wasn't alone out here in the middle of the night. Someone followed me…*pushed* me.

I continue treading water, pushing and pulling

my hands through the lake around my body, kicking harder with my legs to spin myself in a circle. I search the edge of the entire lake, the dock a few feet away, and the path back to the prison. I look for a face hiding in the trees or a glimpse of someone running away, finding nothing but empty land and shadows. My eyes have grown used to the darkness of night but it's hard to see much of anything out here. Yet I know someone is there. I can feel eyes watching me, hiding in the shadows where my vision can't penetrate. Let the bastard watch. See that I can't be gotten rid of this easily. Realize that all that was accomplished by pushing me into the lake was to wake up the corner of my mind that remembers that being in the water makes me feel alive.

Dunking my head backward to smooth my tangled hair out of my face, I twist over onto my stomach and easily slide my arms through the water, right, left, right, keeping my face tilted to the side so I can breathe as I glide smoothly to the east bank of the lake. A few feet before the edge, I dive under, flipping and twisting, pushing off the muddy bottom until I'm zooming back up to the surface in the opposite direction. I swim hard, and I swim perfectly, like I've been doing it all my life, because clearly I have. I swim until the adrenaline from fighting for my life quickly fades away, and I have a hard time keeping my eyes open, even though I want nothing more than to stay in the water forever. I let the sounds of my arms and legs splashing through the water soothe me as I swim to the end of the dock and pull myself up, collapsing on my back on the uneven panels of wood. I gaze up at the stars as I catch my breath, no longer caring if someone is out there watching me, no longer afraid of whoever lurks in the shadows.

"My name is Ravenna Duskin. I'm eighteen years old, I live in a prison, and these secrets and lies will not kill me; they will only make me stronger."

CHAPTER 10

SNEAKING QUIETLY BACK upstairs to my bedroom, I strip out of my sopping wet nightgown and hide it at the bottom of my dirty clothes hamper. Throwing on a dry gown, I grab a towel from the bathroom and tiptoe back downstairs, wiping up the trail of puddles and wet footprints I left behind. I realize what I'm doing is not normal behavior. I know that a normal eighteen-year-old girl, after being shoved by someone into a lake and almost drowning, a week after she suffered an unexplained accident in the woods, would probably be scared to death, running right to her parents and waking them up so they could make everything better.

It's time for me to stop pretending I'm a normal girl, and it's time for me to stop waiting for my parents to be normal parents. They argue and keep secrets, lie to me, and look at me in fear. Nothing about our relationship is normal.

Something clicked inside of me out in that water. For the first time since I woke up confused and disoriented in my bed, I felt alive, and I didn't feel crazy. Something I dreamed of and something I felt deep in my bones turned out to be true. I know how to swim, regardless of what my parents told me, or something I saw written in a photo album. I don't know why I never told them or how I learned without their knowledge or why I let them continue to believe that something that happened to me when I was little still traumatized me today.

It doesn't make sense that not only can I swim, I can swim exceptionally well, like I've been doing it every day of my life. I know I could have swum a hundred more laps and never run out of breath or felt like my arms and legs would turn to jelly. My muscles never grew tired and they never burned like I hadn't used them that way before. My body knew exactly what to do once I forced the panic away. I didn't even have to think about the motions: they came naturally—freestyle, breaststroke, backstroke, diving underwater, and flipping around to push off in the opposite direction. It was exhilarating, and as I swam, I could suddenly picture other times I spent in the water. I couldn't remember everything. I didn't remember where I was or whom I was with; I just remembered being in the water and knowing it was the only place that gave me peace.

There are still so many unanswered questions, but I'm finished trying to make myself believe that my dreams and memories can't possibly be real because they don't make sense. I'm no longer scared of the images and memories that flash through my mind—I crave them. They are the missing pieces, and I know they will all click into place.

After I finish wiping the stairs and the floor, I climb into bed and wince when I flop onto my back. The excitement of realizing I can swim overshadowed the fact that I was pushed into the lake. I didn't imagine the hard shove against my back, and the soreness I currently feel in the center of my spine as I gingerly turn onto my side proves it. Lying here in bed, I think it's pretty telling that my first instinct wasn't to go running to my parents; it was to hide the evidence. The truth of the matter is that I don't trust them. They haven't gone out of their way to figure out what happened to me in the woods, so why would they behave any differently if I told them someone tried to drown me? They would probably tell me I imagined it, remind me my head still isn't quite right, and I should get some more rest and forget all about it.

I should probably be scared that someone was outside in the middle of the night watching me, snuck up behind me, and shoved me into the water. Maybe the culprit is still out there, waiting for another chance to get me alone.

Or maybe the person is right here, under the same roof with me. That thought should petrify me, but it doesn't. Instead, it fills me with anger and determination. I'm not afraid...I'm pissed. Furious that someone thinks I'm weak and won't fight back. Livid that I'm supposed to just accept the lies I'm told as the truth and not question what I feel. Irate that twice now, someone has tried to hurt me and I have no idea who or why.

I close my eyes and drift off to sleep, welcoming the dreams that show me who I really am, letting go of my refusal to believe them.

RUNNING A BRUSH through my high ponytail, I roll my eyes at my reflection in the mirror above my dresser. My mother has no idea I took a pair of scissors to one of my nightgowns and a pair of jeans. She has no idea I walked outside and spoke to Nolan without a bra under the flimsy top and my hair a wild mess around my shoulders. As much as I want to walk around here and flaunt it in my parents' faces that I am not going to cower to them and that I refuse to just accept the things they tell me, I'm not going to just yet. That clothing, along with having my hair wild and free, is one of the few things in my life that feels *right.* As much as I feel better to dress and look like that and as much as it finally makes me feel like *me,* instead of my parents' puppet, I'm not ready to share it with them unless they do something to prove to me without a shadow of a doubt that I can trust them. I don't want them ruining the only thing that makes me feel normal instead of crazy, by taking one look at me and then feeding me more lies about good girls and proper ladies and all the other crap that makes me want to hate them. For now, I'll put on their stupid dresses, and I'll pull my hair back from my face to keep them off my back, even if looking like this makes me miserable.

My parents have their own secrets, and now so do I. Somewhere along the line, I learned how to swim and there has to be a reason why they don't know. Until I have all of the answers, there's no point in sharing anything with them.

A soft knock sounds at my door and I set my brush down before moving to my bed and taking a seat on the edge.

"Come in."

The door opens and my mother steps in, staring down at the floor instead of at me.

"Dr. Beall is here for your check-up," she tells me in a dull monotone voice. "He'll be up soon; he's chatting with your father right now."

She doesn't smile, doesn't come near me for her usual pat on the head, and doesn't flutter about my room, picking up things and putting them away. She also doesn't fill the awkward silence, while we wait for Dr. Beall to make his way up the staircase, with useless, happy chatter about the weather and what her plans are for the day, or suggestions for things I could do to keep me busy. She's been so over the top with her cheerfulness and doing whatever she can to pre-tend that what happened in this room the other day never occurred that I've gotten used to it, and it comes as a complete shock to see her like this. I don't remember ever seeing her without makeup, but it's obvious she isn't wearing any now. I can see the dark circles under her eyes from lack of sleep, and the wrinkles and blemishes that are no longer hidden with her usual thick layer of pan-cake foundation.

For the first time since I can remember, my mother looks old and tired. She looks every bit of her forty years of age, possibly even older than that if I stare at her long enough.

"Is something wrong?" I ask, even though it's glaringly obvious something is wrong with her.

"I'm fine, just feeling under the weather," my mother answers, still not making eye contact.

My dreams last night were filled with pain and hurtful words, scathing looks, disappointment, and outright hatred with flashes of my parents' faces aiming all of this unkindness right at me, their daughter. I can't ignore that and I can't just push aside what I feel deep down inside: that all of this is wrong. My life, my actions, my past…my entire *being* feels wrong and I know it all started the morning I woke up, disoriented and confused. A minor head injury with sporadic memory loss shouldn't make me feel like a completely different person than who I'm supposed to be.

I realize as I stare at my mother that I'm not concerned about her well-being in the least. I'm not worried about her nor do I even care what's going on with her. The only reason I asked if something was wrong is because the silence was getting on my nerves, and I had to say something. I know it's mean and heartless that I don't care about my own mother, but sitting here looking at her, I feel like something shifted inside of me last night and I didn't even fully realize it until just now. Staring at this woman standing in my doorway, I feel nothing but hatred. It's come and gone at different times over the last week and it's always made me feel guilty and ashamed, but not now. I don't even have the desire to try and push it away this time. Just like swimming, it feels *right* and like something I've always done. It feels natural to detest this woman and it makes me feel good. I welcome the anger and the hatred. I crave it, feed off of it, and I'm no longer scared of these feelings.

I barely hear her answer because my mind is occupied with other things. The overwhelming animosity I finally allow to break free and take over, instead of trying to suppress it, makes me feel alive. It makes me want to take it and run with it, revel in it, punish the ones who have hurt me and make them pay. I'm filled with anger and hate; it lives inside of me and I love it. I have always loved it and I've never been ashamed, no matter who tried to make me think otherwise.

"I'm doing this for your own good. It will all be over soon."

My hands clench into fists in my lap, and my fingernails dig painfully into my palms as I imagine what it would be like to punch my mother in the face: the feel of the bones in her nose snapping beneath my knuckles, bright red blood dripping down over her lips and off of her chin. I smile to myself, imagining the feel of that warm, wet liquid dripping down my hands.

I went into the water last night a confused girl who refused to believe the memories that completely differed from everything I've been told about myself. I came out of the water a fighter, letting go of the girl they want me to be because she's dead. She doesn't exist and I'm not sure if she ever did. That cool lake water cleansed me of all my doubt and insecurities. It baptized me anew, and I am never going back.

"You are bad. Bad, bad, bad."

Dr. Beall's footsteps pound up the stairs, and my mother leaves the room without a word.

"My name is Ravenna Duskin. I'm eighteen years old, I live in a prison, and I'm a very bad girl."

CHAPTER 11

"THE CUT ON your head seems to be healing very nicely. How are you sleeping at night? How are the headaches?" Dr. Beall asks as he presses his thumbs gently under my eye and pulls the skin down to look deeper into them.

"I'm sleeping just fine and the headaches are long gone," I tell him with a cheerful smile as he drops his hands from my face and leans back from me.

"Good, very good, Ravenna. Your father tells me you've been acting a little strangely the last few days. Would you like to talk about it?"

The smile drops from my face and I narrow my

eyes at the older man seated on the bed next to me. My father won't speak to *me* about my behavior, but he'll run his mouth to a virtual stranger.

"I'm missing large chunks of my memory—of course I'm acting strange," I tell him in annoyance. "My father seems to think lying to me about everything is the solution to the problem, and I think otherwise."

"If you're still missing pieces of your memories, how do you know your father is lying to you?" he asks calmly, crossing his legs and clasping his hands around his knee.

"I might have forgotten a few things, but that doesn't make me an idiot. The things I *have* remembered are the exact opposite of everything my parents are telling me."

He cocks his head as he studies me, a lock of his white hair falling down over his forehead. "What are they telling you that you don't believe is true?"

I should lie, tell him I'm imagining things so he'll leave and stop studying me like I'm a bug under a microscope. I know as soon as he walks out of my room, he'll tell my father everything we discussed. A few days ago that knowledge would have filled me with dread, but now I no longer care. Let them talk; let my father have another reason to look at me in fear. I'm finished hiding who I am.

"Did you know me before the accident, Dr. Beall?" I ask, pulling my legs under me on the bed and sitting up tall.

"Yes, I've seen you on a few occasions over the years. Little things here and there like the flu, a twisted ankle and other minor problems."

I nod my head and continue. "How would you describe me when you saw me those times?"

His face scrunches up in confusion, but he doesn't say anything about how strange my question is.

"I guess I would say you were a normal, happy young lady. As I said, I didn't have to come out to the prison very often. You were a normal, healthy girl so there was no need for regular check-ups."

There's that word again, *normal*. It's pathetic that it seems to be the common word used to describe me.

"And that seems to be the problem, Doctor. The things I've remembered, the memories that flash through my mind and wake me up in the middle of the night, tell me I was anything but normal. They show me that I probably wasn't the good, perfect little daughter my parents like to keep reminding me of."

Dr. Beall sighs and uncrosses his legs, pushing himself up from my bed to pace around my room.

"The mind is a tricky thing, Ravenna. It gets even more complicated when someone has suffered a head injury as you did. I know it's frustrating, but you can't always believe everything you see when your mind is still in the process of healing," he explains. "Our minds can play tricks on us. Make us see things that aren't really there or feel things we wouldn't normally feel. It doesn't mean your parents are lying to you about anything or that you suddenly woke up a completely different person."

I bite my tongue to stop myself from screaming at him. I want to scramble off the bed and shove his old, slow-moving body right to the floor. I didn't just wake up one morning a different person. I know with everything inside of me that I've *always* been this person. Why else would I feel so alive letting the anger consume me? A switch has been flipped and I no longer care about turning it off because I like feeling strong and in control of my life.

"The night of my accident, did my parents tell you what happened?"

He stops pacing and turns to face me. "Just the basics that I would need to assess the situation. Your father called my home around one in the morning, telling me you'd suffered an accident outside and you weren't conscious. I got dressed and came right over. I checked your injuries, dressed the wound on your head and your mother assisted me in cleaning you up and putting you in dry clothes before we put you to bed. I was told you must have been sleepwalking and fell down out in the woods and your injuries matched that information. When I questioned you after you woke up, you couldn't remember what happened, so there was no reason to think otherwise."

It was pointless thinking this man could give me answers to my questions or fill in any blanks. He's going along with whatever my parents told him and not bothering to think anything is strange about what happened. Why would he? Two seemingly loving parents who run a well-known business in town tell the good doctor their daughter was walking in her sleep and must have been clumsy. When the daughter wakes up and can't confirm or deny their story, there's no reason to argue it.

"Everything is going to be fine, Ravenna, you'll see. Just rest your mind and you'll be back to your old self in no time," he tells me with a smile as he comes back to the bed, closes his black leather medical bag and moves to my door.

"I do believe I'm already back to my old self," I mutter under my breath.

Dr. Beall stops with his hand on the door and looks back at me. "Did you say something, dear?"

I give him a fake smile and shake my head. He nods, pulling open my door and is just stepping out into the living room when another question pops into my mind. I jump up from my bed and jog to the doorway, stopping him at the top of the stairs.

"Dr. Beall, one last thing."

He stops and turns, waiting for me to walk across the room to him.

"When I was little, around five, there was an accident here at the prison. I think it happened out at the lake and, according to my parents, ever since then I've refused to learn how to swim, and I'm terrified of the water," I explain. "Do you remember anything about that? Did my parents call you out here to check on me?"

The doctor scrunches his nose and stares down at the floor while he thinks. After a few seconds, he shakes his head and looks back up at me.

"If I recall, you were around six years of age the first time I ever treated you. Now that I think about it, there used to be a full-time doctor on staff here at the prison. He not only attended to the inmates, but the warden and his family as well. I believe he was the one who delivered you and handled all of your medical care until I took over."

I let out a frustrated breath, realizing I've hit another dead end. Dr. Beall tells me he'll come back to check on me soon, and heads down the stairs. At the bottom, he suddenly stops and turns around.

"I can't believe I forgot about this. It's been so many years since it happened that I guess I pushed it out of my mind," he says with a chuckle as he looks up the stairs at me. "It was such a strange thing…"

I move slowly down the stairs toward him, clutching the banister so I don't tumble to the bottom. I'm lost in his words, eager for the rest of the story, even though something tells me I've heard it before. Something tells me I've *lived* it before.

"He worked here for many years, the doctor, and of course I'd heard of him before. He'd developed a host of new techniques dealing with patients with mental issues, especially those spending time in prison, and he was renowned for his work. He was consumed with dissecting the criminal mind, wanting to know how it ticked, what made them different from the rest of society and what caused them to do such unspeakable things," Dr. Beall explains.

I hold my breath as I continue moving down the stairs, stopping when I'm on the step right above him.

"He thought he could trick a person's brain into behaving differently. That through certain tests and continuous therapies, a robber, for instance, would no longer have the need or the desire to steal things from other people," he explains.

"This hurts me more than it hurts you."

"If you'd stop being bad, I wouldn't have to do this to you."

"Anyway," Dr. Beall continues. "Right before I moved to town and started treating you, the doctor just up and disappeared. No one ever heard from him again. Not his family, not his friends and none of his colleagues. He just vanished and he took all of his medical files with him. Which is why I didn't have much to go on when I first started treating you when you were six. There was no record of your birth or any information about past treatments and I just had to start from scratch."

My hand clutches so tightly to the banister that my knuckles turn white and my arm starts to shake. A sharp shooting pain stabs into my skull and nausea churns in my stomach. My skin breaks out into a cold sweat and before I know it, the shaking in my arm has moved through my entire body.

Don't ask the next question.
Keep your mouth shut and walk away.
Don't ask.
Don't ask.
Don't ask.

"What was the doctor's name?" I whisper, the words leaving my mouth all on their own and I'm unable to stop them.

"His name? It was Thomas. Dr. Raymond Thomas."

"Stop fighting, just let go, it will all be over soon."
"Why do you make me do these things to you?"
"It will only hurt for a little while."
Burn.
Pain.
Stab.
Poke.
Prod.
Just let me go in the water. Why can't I go in the water?
"The water is for good little girls who do as they're told."
I hate you. I'll make you pay. I don't deserve this.
It will all be over soon because I will kill you.

PART VI

Everything around me goes dark and I feel myself falling, mumbling to myself before I let go.

"My name is Ravenna Duskin. I'm eighteen years old, I live in a prison, and I'm full of hate."

CHAPTER 12

"I 'LL BE GOOD, *I promise!*"

I scream and claw and fight at the arms wrapped around my small body, but it's no use. They don't love me. They never loved me. They're tossing me away like garbage.

"This is for your own good."

I hate them, I hate them, I hate them.

"Please don't make me go!"

I bite down hard on the arm around my neck, dragging me away. My teeth pierce the skin and blood fills my mouth.

The shouts of pain, curses, and yells are muffled, and I barely hear them. The warm metallic taste in my mouth fills me with hunger and rage.

I laugh when I'm roughly shoved away and smile when my body hits the ground. They stare at me in fear and horror and it makes me happy. I can feel the blood dripping down my chin and I lick it away like a drop of ice cream.

"You are a bad little girl."

This time, I let them yank me up from the ground and pull me away. I'll come back, and I'll make them pay. They did this to me, and they will pay.

My eyes pop open and I have to blink a few times to make them adjust to the dark. I feel blankets around my body and a pillow under my head and realize I'm in my bed, my dresser and the open door to my bathroom coming into focus in the shadows. I lie here for a few minutes, letting myself fully wake up before I start thinking about what happened.

I was talking to Dr. Beall. He said something I didn't like. It made me remember something, but what was it? I close my eyes and picture myself standing on the stairs, looking down at the doctor. He was telling me a story, and it was about my childhood. I remember feeling sick to my stomach, and I wanted to make him stop talking, but I couldn't.

A name! He said a name and I hated it. Just the sound of it made me feel like someone was hurting me. I squeeze my eyes closed tighter, trying to pluck the name forward, trying to keep picturing myself on those stairs but everything in my head suddenly disappears like a brick wall has slammed down, blocking me from what I need.

The hairs on the back of my neck suddenly rise and my eyes fly open, realizing I'm not alone in my dark, quiet room. I slowly roll over and turn my head to the side, my heart pounding in my chest when I see a dark figure standing next to my bed staring down at me. It makes me remember that night in the woods, lying on the muddy, wet ground and looking up to see a shadow hovering over me. Is it the same person here to finish what he or she started?

"I'm sorry. I'm so sorry."

The words are soft, barely a whisper of sound, and my heart thumps loudly in my chest. I remain perfectly still in my bed as the shadow leans closer, the light from the moon shining through my window finally allowing me to make out who it is.

"I didn't know. I'm sorry," my mother whispers again.

Her voice is full of anguish, and I hear her sniffle and realize she's crying.

She doesn't move any closer, just continues to stand in the shadows staring down at me.

"It's my fault. It's all my fault. I was so weak and he was so strong," she rambles quietly. "I made a mistake, and everyone suffered. I didn't know. You have to believe me, I didn't know."

I stay quiet and still, letting her unload her guilt and make her confessions, even though I have no idea what she's rambling about.

Gazing at her in the darkness, I watch as she turns away from me, moving to the window to stare out into the night in a daze. The moonlight illuminates her profile, and I see tears fall like a river down her cheeks. I notice that she's clutching something in her hands, holding it against her chest, but the light from the moon isn't strong enough for me to make out what it is.

"My daughter, so beautiful and perfect and good.

I'm so sorry. I shouldn't have believed him. I should have seen the truth all along. It hurts so much. Oh my God, it hurts. I deserve this; I understand that now."

So far, that's the only statement she's made that I can understand and agree with. The secrets, the lies, the dreams and memories I have of so much pain…she was the cause of it. She and my father both were, and they deserve to suffer as much as I have.

"I have to make this right. I have to stop the pain," she whispers, bringing one hand up to swipe away the tears.

With her palm pressed against her cheek, the moonlight glints off the object still clutched in her other hand against her chest and I can clearly make out what it is now.

I jerk my body up and kick the covers off me, scrambling off of my bed on the opposite side of where my mother stands, moving so quickly that I stumble to the ground, my knees smacking roughly against the hardwood.

My mother doesn't pay me any attention; she just continues to stare out the window. The only movement she makes is to pull the object away from her chest, pressing the length against the side of her head, pointing it up at the ceiling.

I should be afraid that my mother came into my room in the middle of the night, mumbling nonsense as she holds a gun in her hand. I should scream for my father, shout for help, run out of the room as fast as I can. Clutching onto the edge of my mattress, I slowly push myself up from the floor and face her head on. She looks so sad and full of apology, small and miserable with her shoulders sagging in defeat, and I smile in the darkness that she's falling apart right in front of my eyes. I ran away that night in the woods and look where it got me? A fractured mind that no one wants to help me fix. I refuse to run away this time.

I'm not scared of this pathetic woman; my head is too busy filling with memories of her looks of disgust, the slap of her hand, the vitriol she screamed at me, the blame she placed on my shoulders for the actions *she* was responsible for, and how easily she could pretend like I didn't exist.

My heart doesn't beat in fear: it thumps in anger. How dare she come in here, dumping her guilt all over me to try and clear her conscience? She's had plenty of time to make amends and now that the truth is unraveling, now that I'm starting to put things together and refuse to believe their lies, she decides it's time for honesty.

"You never loved me," I finally speak.

She doesn't move or make any indication that she heard me. My memory is still spotty, large chunks of time are still unaccounted for, but I know the words I say are true. I can feel their certainty ringing through my mind just like it did with knowing I can swim.

For days I tried to tell myself my memories were wrong. It made more sense that I might be crazy than to think my entire life is a lie and my parents were just perpetuating it.

"It was me out by the lake," she whispers, ignoring my statement.

She suddenly throws her head back and laughs, the sound bouncing off the walls in my small room.

"I had to see. I had to know for sure and I was right."

My mouth drops open in shock, not at her admittance of what she did, but the sound of glee in her voice.

"You pushed me in the lake," I mutter through clenched teeth. "What exactly did you have to know for sure? If you had the courage to try and kill your own daughter?"

My body vibrates with rage and I want to vault over my bed, wrap my hands around her neck and squeeze and squeeze until her face turns red and every last breath leaves her body. I keep my feet firmly planted where they are because right now I want the truth more than I want to hurt her.

My mother lets out a huge, tired sigh and finally turns to look at me, carelessly waving the gun around by her head.

"I'm sorry you had to pay for my sins and my weakness," she tells me in a robotic voice. "I just had to see. I had to know for sure that I was right. I felt bad as soon as I saw you go under, wondering if I'd made a mistake, but I didn't. You came up and you proved me right. I ignored what was right in front of my face because I just wanted it so badly. I was blind and I was stupid, but I'm going to fix all of it now."

She speaks so quickly that it's hard for me to keep up, but I do, and I get the truth I've been waiting for. My own mother tried to drown me. I glare across my bed at her, refusing to cower when she turns the gun and aims it right at my chest.

"I'm sorry. This is the only way I know how to fix things. This is the only way I can stop the pain," she tells me sadly.

"You are a *coward*," I growl at her. "You are weak and pathetic. You can apologize all you want, but it means nothing to me. I've remembered things on my own, no thanks to you and Dad. I drove myself crazy with the thoughts in my head that didn't match the lies you both told me. The only thing you accomplished by pushing me into the lake was waking me up to the person I really am. I deserve the truth, *Mother*."

Her hold on the gun falters and it lowers a few inches, pointing at the bed instead of me. Knowing I have a little more time before everything ends pushes me to keep going.

"I deserve to know why all I can remember is pain and hate when this house is filled with happy memories of a loving family that obviously never existed.

Tell me the truth. TELL ME THE DAMN TRUTH! ALL OF IT!" I shout in fury.

She whimpers painfully, bringing the gun back up where it was.

"It was real… all of it was real. We were happy… we were so happy. I made up for my mistakes and everything was perfect… everything was just as it should be. I should have known better. Secrets never stay hidden no matter how deep you bury them. Mistakes will always come back to haunt you and get their revenge."

Her body is wracked with sobs, her shoulders shaking with the force of her cries, each breath out of her mouth punctuated with whimpers and mournful whines.

"My perfect, beautiful daughter. I can't do this anymore. It hurts too much. You need to find him. You need to talk to him. You'll see him, and you'll understand. It will all make sense then," she cries.

"I need to find who? Dr. Thomas?" I ask, vomit rising up my throat as soon as I speak his name, the name Dr. Beall said to me, the one my mind wouldn't let me remember just moments ago when I woke up. It flies off my tongue with ease, and I hate it. I hate the name. I hate the person. I don't want to remember.

Go away, go away, go away!

"He only did what we asked. We thought it was right. We thought it would make everything better," she whimpers.

My hands come up to my head and my fingers clutch tightly to my hair, yanking it as hard as I can until the pain brings tears to my eyes. I need the pain. I need the hurt. It's the only way I can think clearly. Nothing she says makes any sense. She's talking in circles, and I want to scream in frustration.

"I always loved the picture your father has of our family that sits on the desk in his office," she says in a faraway voice, her crying coming to an abrupt end as an eerie smile takes over her face. "The picture tells the truth. It knows all the secrets."

Maybe I really *am* crazy and I inherited it from my mother. She is out of her mind.

Her eyes meet mine across the bed, and as I stare into them, I see nothing but glazed-over emptiness. I'm not even sure if she realizes the crazy things she's said to me or if she's so far gone that they all make sense in her twisted mind.

"I can't live without you. I can't pretend anymore. I need to be wherever you are but I don't even know where that is," she complains, her eyes staring right through me. "He lies. He lies, and he lies, and he won't tell me, but I deserve it. He tried to fix what I did but it didn't work. I'm you, and you're me. We're so alike that no amount of lying can change that. No more pain, no more lying. Talk to the picture, and listen to what it says."

My mother sniffs loudly and swipes away the last

of her tears. She wraps both hands around the gun to hold it steady, out in front of her body.

I let go of the mattress and drop my arms to my sides. I refuse to close my eyes. I want her to suffer as she stares into mine, the exact same shade of emerald green as hers. I want her to watch the life she gave me vanish from my eyes, and I want it to kill everything inside of her, knowing that this is all her fault.

"I love you, Ravenna. I love you more than you could possibly imagine, and I'm so sorry. We'll be together again soon. Wait for me."

Faster than I can take my next breath, she bends her elbows back, sticks the end of the gun in her mouth, and pulls the trigger. My hands fly up to cover my ears but I'm not fast enough. The loud explosion in such a small space rings through my ears, and I wince in pain, pressing my palms as hard as I can against the side of my head to make the pain stop.

My eyes are glued to my mother's lifeless body until she slumps to the ground and disappears from sight on the other side of my bed. My gaze slowly tracks up the wall where she was standing just moments ago, stopping at the hole at the top of my bedroom window where the bullet must have gone after it exited the back of her head.

The room suddenly fills with bright light, illuminating every corner of the room, the dark shadows no longer able to hide what happened in here. I drop my hands from my ears, and my father's screams suddenly surround me. I feel his hands wrap around my arms as he jerks my body around to face him, but my eyes never leave the hole in the window. I stare in fascination at the dark, wet splatters of dripping blood and pieces of my mother's brains as they slide down the glass and splat on the floor.

"My name is Ravenna Duskin. I'm eighteen years old, I live in a prison, and my mother is dead."

CHAPTER 13

"YOU'RE SURE YOU'RE okay that your dad didn't want to have a funeral?"

With my legs dangling over the end of the dock, I kick them lazily back and forth, staring at my reflection in the water below.

"What would be the point, Nolan?" I ask with a shrug. "It's not like we have any family that would attend. My parents were both only children and my grandparents have been dead for years. My father also didn't really want to advertise the fact that my mother swallowed a bullet. Not very good for the perfect little reputation he's built around here."

I laugh at my own joke, but Nolan just sighs in sympathy.

It's been a week since my mother shot herself in my bedroom and a week of being ignored by my father while he locked himself in his office and sucked down one bottle of whiskey after another. The only reason I know what he's doing behind that closed door is because each time he'd finish a bottle, he'd open his office door just wide enough for the bottle to fit through, clunk it down roughly on the floor, and then slam the door closed.

When I walked by the door on my way out here to the lake, I counted six empty bottles all in a clump right outside the door. I'm assuming he's shoving them out of his office because his drunken mind thinks I'll pick up where my mother left off and clean up after him. He can just keep right on assuming that because it will be a cold day in hell before I do anything for that man.

"I've never noticed that birthmark before."

Nolan's finger gently traces over the crescent moon-shaped birthmark the size of a fifty-cent piece on my upper thigh and goose bumps pebble my skin at his soft touch.

Swatting his hand away, I shrug and turn my face toward the sun. "I've had it since birth, hence, the name *birthmark*."

He chuckles, and I close my eyes, instead of rolling them in annoyance that he didn't notice the sarcastic bite to my words.

"Has your dad spoken to you yet?" he asks as he leans back on his hands, tilts his head up toward the sun, and closes his eyes.

"Nope."

Pulling my legs up onto the dock, I twist my body to face Nolan, crisscrossing my legs in front of me.

"He said plenty to me the night she shot herself. I would be perfectly fine if he never spoke to me again," I tell him, thinking about how my father cradled my mother's body in his arms, screaming accusations and hatred at me. Even though it was obvious I didn't pull the trigger, and I didn't force my mother to do what she did, according to my father, it was still my fault. He cried and screamed, he mumbled nonsense, and then he screamed some more. When I got tired of listening to him, I walked out of the room and left him alone with his anger and misery.

"I know I've already said this, but I'm sorry for what's happening to you," he tells me softly.

"It's not your fault. Right now, the only thing I care about is remembering what happened that night in the woods because I feel like it all started that night. Why was I out there? Who was out there with me, and how did I get back up to the prison?"

Nolan is silent and I turn my head to look at him. He's looking off in the opposite direction, lost in thought.

"You didn't hear anything about that night, right?

Like, maybe some of the workers were here and saw something?"

He shakes his head, but still doesn't turn to face me. I start to call him on it when he suddenly turns and leans toward me.

"You know I care about you, right? And I'd never let anything happen to you?" he asks.

I nervously rub my hands up and down my arms, feeling agitated by what his words do to me. Nolan and I have spent every day together since my mother's death. Because my father has locked himself in his office, he hasn't given the grounds crew a list of jobs that needs to be done, like he usually does every morning when they get here. After the first day when they finished with all of the obvious things that needed taking care of, they didn't figure it would make sense to come all the way out here and have nothing to do. They left, telling me to have my father call them when he wanted them to come back to work.

Much to my surprise, when I woke up the following morning and came outside for some air, Nolan was sitting on the top step of the porch waiting for me. I tried to brush him off, ignore him in the hopes that he'd go away, but he wouldn't give up that easily. I didn't want to like him. I didn't have time to waste looking forward to his visits. I was too consumed with my newly discovered personality, enjoying the thrill of behaving however I pleased, without having to worry about consequences. I still had secrets to uncover and memories to remember and being with Nolan was simply not on the agenda.

I thought it would be easy to push him aside because I didn't like the way he made me feel. When he spoke to me so soft and sweet, when he looked at me like he was interested in what I had to say, it scared me deep down to the very core of me. I wasn't afraid of being chased through the woods, almost drowned, and having my mother aim a loaded gun at my chest. I'm not afraid of my memories that show me the horrible things that were done to me, the awful words that were said to me, and I know I won't be afraid of what's yet to come, when it all clicks into place and everything makes sense. All of those things strengthen me and push me to keep going, get to the bottom of everything, and show them all, whoever they are, that they can't ignore me any longer.

One look, one word, one brush of Nolan's hand along my bare arm, and I want to get up and run as far away as possible. I hate the way he makes me feel, but at the same time, I crave it. I realized my fear comes from being afraid of the unknown. No one has ever looked at me like he does, no one has ever spoken to me like he does, and I don't know how to handle it. I can easily deal with the anger and hatred, the pain and misery. I'm used to those things: they're a part of me and the more they're thrown in my direction, the stronger I feel and the harder I fight.

I don't know how to deal with someone being

genuinely nice to me. It's foreign, and it's strange, and it puts me on edge. After two days of trying my hardest to pick fights with Nolan by calling him names, belittling him, shoving my hands against his chest, and doing whatever I could to try and get a rise out of him, I finally had to give up and just deal with the discomfort.

Instead of answering his question about knowing if he cares for me and that he wouldn't let anything happen to me, I change the subject before I do something stupid and pathetic like cry.

"I need your help with something today," I tell him, pushing myself up from the dock to stand over him.

He shields his eyes from the sun as he looks up at me. "Please tell me you need help moving out of your room."

I smile and hold my arm out toward him. He wraps his warm callused hand around mine and I pull to help him up, quickly dropping his hand when he's standing in front of me before it makes me feel like running in the opposite direction. I need the use of his muscles today, and I don't have time to run away like a child.

"As a matter of fact, I do," I tell him as we walk back up to the prison.

Nolan has been begging me for days to move out of my bedroom and into the spare room. He is completely grossed out that my mother's blood still stains the window and walls of my room, and he doesn't understand why I continue to sleep there every night.

Even with my confusion and overall uneasy feelings about being treated with kindness and respect, there's still something about Nolan that makes it impossible for me to shut my mouth when I'm with him. He's easy to talk to, and he never once looks at me in disgust or judgment when I speak to him, even when I've told him some of the more strange and awful things I've remembered. I told him about my dreams, the flashes of memories, the realization that something very bad happened to me growing up, and even everything my mother said to me before she took her own life.

If he isn't going to leave me alone and I'm going to continue being a glutton for punishment by hanging around him, the least he could do is help me figure everything out and try to make sense of the things my mother told me. As we walk side-by-side through the grass up to the front porch, just remembering how everything unfolded that night makes my breath come out in short, angry pants. My hatred for her grows even stronger when I replay the drivel that came out of her mouth, not even having the decency to finally tell me everything I was missing before she selfishly shot herself. Instead, she spoke in riddles that didn't make sense and now became yet another puzzle I'd have to figure out. I stomp so hard up the stairs, I'm surprised the old wood doesn't crumble beneath my feet.

Nolan puts his hand on my arm, stopping me when we get to the top of the stairs. "Are you okay?"

I quickly wipe the anger from my face, shaking out my clenched hands, and smile up at him.

"Perfectly fine," I reassure him.

I've opened myself up to Nolan, more than I felt comfortable with, but I drew the line at letting him in on the thoughts and feelings that run through me and stimulate me. A girl needs to have a few secrets and something tells me that informing Nolan I dream of blood and death and fantasize about revenge and hate and hurting people wouldn't go over very well. Maybe I'll tell him everything some day. Maybe when I'm finished using him to help me uncover the missing pieces, and I no longer need him, I'll show him who I really am.

Nolan jogs across the porch and opens the front door, holding it wide so I can enter. I walk past him and continue moving toward the stairs, making it halfway up when I realize he's not following behind me. Looking over my shoulder, I find him standing awkwardly at the base of the stairs with his hands in his pocket.

"If you're going to help me switch rooms, it would help if you're actually *in* the rooms with me," I remind him.

He still doesn't move up the stairs toward me. Instead, his eyes dart nervously around the hallway and then beyond me up the stairs.

"What's the problem?" I ask, trying not to let my irritation show.

"I've never been upstairs in the living quarters before," he tells me.

"Okaaaaaaay," I reply, drawing the word out in confusion.

He huffs out an irritated breath, pulling his hands out of his pockets to cross his arms in front of him. "Look, this is a little weird, even knowing your father is probably comatose in his office. He doesn't like me, I don't like him, and he would kill me if he found me upstairs. If he found me upstairs in your *bedroom*, he would revive me just so he could kill me again."

I laugh, rolling my eyes at him.

"Stop being such a chicken. You have no reason to be afraid of him," I tell him, turning back around to continue upstairs.

"Don't be a chicken, you knew this day would come. You should have spent more time being afraid of me, instead of hurting me."

I stop suddenly on the stairs, not realizing Nolan finally followed until he bumps into my back. He asks me something but I block him out, trying to concentrate. I close my eyes, repeating the words that just popped into my head, over and over, hoping to retrieve something else along with them. Did I say them? Did someone say them to me? Where was I?

How old was I?

Just like always, my mind shuts down like someone slammed a door in my face. I let out a frustrated sigh and open my eyes, continuing the rest of the way up the stairs.

"Did you remember something else?" Nolan asks softly as he moves next to me when we get to the top.

I wave him off with my hand and head to my bedroom.

"Nothing important," I lie, entering my room and taking a look around, trying to figure out what to move first.

"Good God," Nolan mutters, stopping in the doorway.

His eyes are wide and his hand comes up to cover his mouth. I open my own to ask him what his problem is, quickly snapping it shut when I realize that little trip down memory lane distracted me so much that I almost forgot Nolan has never been up here before. I'm so used to staring at the huge dark stain on my window and walls that I forgot it would probably be disturbing to someone else. I wait for him to ask me why I haven't at least tried to wash some of it off, especially the window where most of the blood and pieces of brain matter landed.

He walks up next to me and puts his arm around my shoulder, giving it a gentle squeeze. "This is awful, Ravenna, I'm so sorry. If you want to go in the other room, I'll clean it up and get everything out of here, so you don't have to be in this room any longer."

I try not to fidget uncomfortably with the heavy weight of his arm over my shoulder, and I press my lips together tightly before I'm tempted to admit everything to him. I let him continue to assume I've been so distraught that I couldn't bring myself to wash away the evidence of what my mother did. It's probably best I don't tell him that I never washed the window and wall because lying here in bed at night with my bright overhead light on, it calms me to stare at the mess my mother left behind. It helps me fall asleep staring at the dark red splatter, trying to find hidden shapes in the dried splotches.

The only reason I'm moving out of this bedroom is because it represents everything I'm not. It's a daily reminder of the girl my parents tried to fool me into being. And I'm getting tired of Nolan begging me to move out several times a day.

I shrug out from under his arm and move over to my dresser. "I'm fine, Nolan, really. Let's just get this done so we can move on to more important things."

I open a drawer and start pulling everything out of it while Nolan goes to the bed, sliding the top mattress off and tipping it to the side before pushing it across the floor to the door.

"So what's the plan? I've been thinking about everything you told me and I can't make sense of any of it," he tells me as he pushes the mattress out of the doorway and into the living room.

I dump the pile of clothes in my arms onto the floor and follow him out so I can point out which room I'm moving to. I walk along the tipped mattress he holds up and stop short in front of the spare room.

"Shit. I forgot the door is locked," I complain.

Nolan leans the mattress against the back of the couch and comes up next to me. He squats down and studies the doorknob for a few seconds. The doors and matching hardware up in our living quarters are still the originals from when the prison was first built. The knob is made of thick glass, framed with an oblong brass filigree backplate that requires a skeleton key to open—a skeleton key that is on a key ring in my father's locked office.

"What kind of clothing hangers do you have in your closet?" Nolan asks, tilting his head to the side as he studies the lock hole.

"Just regular wire ones I guess."

"Can you grab me one please?" he asks. "I think I might be able to pick this thing."

Jogging back to the room, I grab a hanger from the pole in my closet and hurry back to Nolan. Taking the hanger from me, I watch as he unbends the curved top of the hanger until it's pointing straight out. He sticks the end into the keyhole, and after a few minutes of jiggling it around inside, as well as a couple of muttered curses under his breath, I hear a loud *click*. Nolan stands, tossing the hanger to the side, and turns the handle, pushing the door open.

I smile up at him as I walk by. "A gentleman *and* a handyman. Very nice."

He returns my smile, and I quickly look away before I start to like it too much.

My feet suddenly come to a stop in the middle of the room when I see a dark blue hard-side leather suitcase with white trim, lying on its side in the middle of the bed. This time, I don't even need to concentrate to pull the memory into focus. It slides right into place in my mind like it's always been there and I move to the bed silently, running my hand over the side of the familiar piece of luggage.

"This will be your room. Dinner is in an hour, so you can hang up your things in the closet while you wait. You will be on time and you will respect the rules while you're under this roof. You have one chance to prove yourself. Screw it up, and you will regret it."

Tossing my luggage onto the neatly made bed, I wisely keep my mouth shut as he turns and leaves the room, slamming the door closed behind him.

"Thanks for the lovely welcome, Ike. We'll see who's the first to have regrets," I mutter under my breath before flopping on top of the bed.

I bounce a few times on the mattress while I look around the room. It's different from what I remember but that's no surprise. Of course they'd erase every trace of their mistake as soon as it was out of sight.

Shoving my suitcase out of the way, I lie on my back with my hands behind my head and stare up at the ceiling, having no intention of unpacking my things. They'll find out soon enough that I'm not going to follow their rules.

Closing my eyes, I go over the plan once more in my head. I can't make any mistakes because it has to be perfect.

"Perfect, perfect, perfect," I whisper softly.

I smile to myself when I finish chanting their favorite word.

"Enjoy your little perfection while you can, because I'm going get rid of it, once and for all."

Grabbing the handle of the suitcase, I pull it to the edge of the bed and move my hands to either end of it, flipping open the gold snaps holding it closed.

I feel Nolan come up behind me, the front of his body brushing up against my back while he silently looks over my shoulder. The lid of the suitcase creaks as I slowly open it, staring down at the contents with a smile on my face.

"Why did you put all of *these* clothes in a suitcase in another room and keep the stuffy, boring dresses in your closet?" he asks in confusion.

Glancing down at myself and the one pair of jean shorts I hacked off, paired with one of the "stuffy" dresses I turned into a crop top by cutting it off from the waist down, I smile as I look back inside the suitcase.

I hated those dresses, but I put them on every day because I was told they were what I loved and what I always wore. I forced myself to accept what I was told, even though it didn't feel right, and I didn't recognize the girl in the mirror.

"I have no idea," I finally answer Nolan as I pull every item out of the suitcase.

This time, I don't really have to lie to him. I remember being in this room, and I knew what would be in this suitcase before I even opened it, but I still don't remember anything else.

Right now, it doesn't matter. Pulling out ratty and well-worn jean shorts, miniskirts and tank tops, bell-bottoms and crop tops, I spread them out all over the bed and stare at the items before me. Confidence flares inside me with the knowledge that yet another gut feeling I had that conflicted with what my parents told me turned out to be correct.

"My name is Ravenna Duskin. I'm eighteen years old, I live in a prison, and I can finally dress the way I'm supposed to."

CHAPTER 14

PACING BACK AND forth in the hallway while I wait for Nolan to get here, I try to come up with a way to get my father out of his office. I need to get in there and look at the picture my mother mentioned. I'm sure most of what she said to me that night in my room was utter nonsense from a delusional woman, but maybe not all of it. I won't know for sure until I can get to the picture and see if it makes me remember anything.

There's a knock at the door, and I race over to it and quickly throw it open. My shoulders drop and I let out an annoyed sigh, leaning my shoulder against the doorjamb and crossing my arms over my chest.

"What are you doing here?"

Trudy stands in front of me with her long blonde hair curled up at the ends and a wide yellow headband keeping her bangs pulled back on top of her head. She's wearing a short yellow dress with a full skirt and capped sleeves, like a perfect ray of sunshine. It's so pathetic I want to throw up on her black and white saddle shoes. Maybe *she's* really my parents' long-lost daughter. She certainly dresses the part.

Trudy holds out a bright orange Pyrex dish with a daisy painted on the white lid and smiles brightly.

"We just heard about your mom. I'm so sorry, Ravenna. My mom made a tuna casserole for you and your father. You haven't returned any of my calls lately so I thought we could hang out and talk."

Keeping my arms crossed, I stare down at the dish in disgust. "Thanks, but no thanks."

I push off the doorframe, stepping back inside to close the door in her face. Trudy moves fast, sticking her foot in front of the door to stop it from closing.

"Look, I know your mom died, but that's no reason for you to be so nasty to me when I'm just trying to help," she says, tucking the dish under one arm. "What's happened to you lately, Ravenna? One minute you're my friend, then you're mean to me, then you're normal, and now you're back to acting weird."

She pauses in the middle of her speech to look me up and down from head to toe. "Also, that outfit you're wearing is trashy."

Maybe the black high-waist shorts that barely cover my butt and dark blue crop tank top that shows off a strip of the pale skin of my stomach are a bit much when I'm just going to be wandering around a prison all day, but this is who I am and Miss Trudy Sunshine better watch her mouth.

"Have you even brushed your hair in a week?" she finishes haughtily.

"What's your problem, Ravenna? You look awful.

Have you even brushed your hair in a week?"

A slow smile spreads across my face as I stare at the simpering idiot standing in front of me. This might be one of the best parts of my plan. If I'm going to destroy it all, might as well start with the useless best friend.

"He doesn't want you. You realize that, right? You're just a sad, pathetic little girl who can't handle it when someone else has something you want."

Her attitude vanishes and she drops her hands from her hips.

"W-what are you talking about?" she nervously stutters.

I laugh right in her face. How in the world would someone ever want to be friends with a girl who is so clueless?

"I saw you from my bedroom window, Trudy. Just because a guy feels sorry for you and spends a few minutes talking to you, doesn't mean he wants you to throw yourself at him."

She rubs her hands together in front of her worriedly.

"You saw us together?" she whispers in shock.

"If by together you mean mauling the poor guy in a sad attempt at trying to kiss him while he stood there with his arms out to the side and a horrified look in his eyes, then yes. I saw you together. Thanks for giving me something to laugh about for a few hours," I tell her with a chuckle.

"You are a horrible person, Ravenna Duskin," she tells me as her eyes well up with tears. You're just jealous because he likes me."

I throw my head back and laugh again. I laugh so hard and for so long that my stomach starts to ache. When the laughter subsides, I take a step toward her and get right up in her face.

"You're just like every other whore, trying to take what isn't yours. No one is falling for that innocent act you put on, you snobby, lying bitch."

Her eyes widen in fear and it sends a thrill through my body. I want to claw at her perfect face and her perfect skin until blood drips down onto her perfect pink dress and ruins it. I want to rip every strand of her perfect blonde hair out of her perfect ponytail until she runs away screaming in pain. My hands start to shake and butterflies flap with excitement in my stomach.

She moves away from me, but she isn't fast enough. My arm slices through the air and my nails scratch down the side of her neck. She lets out a yelp of shock and pain, her hand flying up to press against the angry red marks I left behind.

"You just scratched my neck!" she cries, her lower lip quivering as she quickly backs farther and farther away from me.

"Lucky you. I was aiming for your face."

I stand in the hallway with a smile on my face, watching her turn and race out the front door as fast as she can.

"Hello? Ravenna? Did you even hear me?"

Blinking my eyes into focus, I glance at the side of Trudy's neck, but sadly the marks from my nails have healed.

"So how's the new kitten? Does she still have really sharp claws?" I ask with a raise of my eyebrow.

Her hand unconsciously comes up to the side of her neck, dropping it quickly when she realizes I'm staring at that spot, sad that evidence of my anger is long gone.

"I thought you couldn't remember anything?" she asks reproachfully.

"Not everything. Not yet. Just a few things, like how you tried to steal Nolan from me."

I'd like to take a moment to appreciate the fire I see in her eyes and her attempt at having a backbone, but she's too stupid of a human being for me to waste that on.

"Oh, give me a break," she scoffs. "You spent two years wanting nothing to do with him just because he was a gardener and too far beneath your social standards. The minute I show interest in him, suddenly you're dressing like a slut and throwing yourself at him."

I move right up in front of her until she has no choice but to take a few steps back, moving herself out of the doorway and back onto the porch.

"Did you know Ike has been missing for a few weeks? And my mother just died. Haven't seen my father around in a few days either," I muse, tapping a finger against my chin. "Strange how people around here disappear or end up dead, don't you think?"

Trudy's face turns as white as a sheet and without another word, she runs as fast as possible down the stairs and over to the driveway, jumping into her father's Buick Electra. She doesn't even waste time turning the car around; she just guns it backward down the long, winding drive.

Swiping my hands together like I just took out the trash, I close the front door and resume my pacing. My eyes wander to the basement door and I stop when a conversation flutters through my mind.

"Come on, let's go into the basement."

"Are you crazy? It's scary down there."

"It's not scary when you go with someone else. Come on, there's something I want to show you."

"I've been down there before. Believe me, there's nothing I haven't seen."

"You haven't seen the bones…"

My feet carry me to the door as I try to remember more of the conversation. Who was I talking to? It must have been Trudy. Maybe I should have been a little nicer to her for a few more minutes and gotten some answers out of her. I try the handle and just like before, it's still locked. I growl in frustration and it only takes me a second to remember something.

"You are such an idiot, Ravenna," I mumble, running back down the hallway and up the stairs.

Shooting a dirty look at my father's closed office door as I move past it, I scoop up the bent hanger that

I left on the floor right outside the spare bedroom where Nolan tossed it there the other day. Heading back downstairs to the basement door, I slide to a stop across the hardwood in my stocking feet. Squatting down, I shove the end of the hanger into the keyhole and jiggle it around just like I saw Nolan do. I poke and jab, turning the hanger this way and that, quickly growing frustrated that picking a skeleton-key lock isn't as easy as Nolan made it look. I keep working but after a few minutes, my fingers start to cramp from holding the piece of wire and trying to force it in the right spot.

Blowing my hair out of my eyes, I move the hanger into my left hand, shaking out the right to give it a little break before going right back to work. I'm pushing so hard in every direction in the tiny hole that the hanger starts to bend and still the door remains locked.

I *need* to get in that basement. I have to go down there. I don't need to make sense of the things my mother told me. I don't need to get into my father's office. All the answers are down there—I know they are.

"Don't go down there. You'll never come up if you go down there."

I quickly jump up away from the door guiltily, the wire hanger falling from my hands and clattering on the floor.

My father leans against the banister of the stairs,

still wearing the same dark blue suit pants and white button-down from the day the coroner came to take my mother's body away. After a week of wearing and sleeping in the same clothes, they're now wrinkled, stained, and disheveled. One end of his shirt has come un-tucked from his pants and it hangs down over his belt and his short dark hair stands on end all around his head like he's been constantly tugging on clumps of it.

I notice a half-empty bottle of whiskey dangles between two of his fingers down by his thigh and I roll my eyes. It's a wonder he hasn't drunk himself to death yet.

"Did you hear me, little girl? Don't go down those stairs," he slurs, swaying away from the banister.

I ignore his warning and shake my head at him. "You might want to try sobering up and taking a shower. The grounds crew hasn't been here in days because they don't know what they're supposed to do and people keep calling about when we're opening back up for tours."

He stares at me without blinking, bringing the bottle up to his lips, tipping it back, and taking a huge swallow.

"You killed her," he whispers as he takes the bottle away from his mouth.

"I didn't kill her. She stuck the gun in her mouth all by herself," I remind him.

He shakes his head and his face scrunches up in

misery. "No, no, no. It was your fault. You killed her. Oh God, what am I going to do? It will kill her if she finds out. I have to hide it—I can't let her know."

Has everyone around me gone mad?

He stumbles forward, his feet shuffling across the floor until he's standing right in front of me. He smells of sweat, whiskey, and vomit, and I scrunch up my nose in disgust as I look up at him.

I used to think he was such a strong, powerful man. I would have done anything to make him love me. Now he's just a sorry excuse for a human being, blaming everyone else for his problems.

His hand suddenly comes up and he cups my cheek in his palm, moving his thumb back and forth softly against my face.

"I'm sorry this happened to you. Come back to me. Please come back to me," he sobs.

Smacking his hand away in frustration and tired of listening to the drunken nonsense coming out of his mouth, I move around him and head toward the door.

"Where are you going? You can't leave. Don't leave me!" he shouts.

"Clean yourself up for God's sake," I yell back, opening the front door.

Hurling his words at my back, he yells, "You're going to see that good-for-nothing boy, aren't you? Did he tell you? I knew he wouldn't be able to keep his mouth shut."

I pause with my hand on the door, turning back around.

"What in the hell are you talking about?" I ask through clenched teeth.

"I've seen you sneaking around with him. I know you've been talking. I should have known better than to trust him with a secret like that, good-for-nothing piece of trash."

He brings the whiskey up to his lips and gulps it down while he moves around the banister and clumsily makes his way back upstairs.

"Tell him he's fired," my father yells down to me. "And tell him he should have minded his own business and stayed out of the woods that night."

CHAPTER 15

*R*AIN SPLASHES DOWN *on my face and I slowly open my eyes, whimpering loudly at the stabbing pain in my head. It's so dark, and everything hurts. I don't know where I am; I don't know what happened, and I don't understand why I'm so wet and cold. I wish I could stop shivering because it just makes everything hurt worse.*

I hear a noise close by, but my head hurts too much to turn it to the side to see what it is. I stare up at the black nothingness above me, wondering if this is a dream, hoping I'll wake up soon so the knives stop stabbing into my head. I don't know where I am. I don't know what's going on, and trying to think just makes my head hurt worse. I feel something slide under my legs and my back, and all of a sudden, I'm floating through the air. I cry out in pain as my body is jostled, not even caring what's happening or where I'm going because at least I'm pressed up against something warm, instead of lying on the cold ground. A bright flash of light illuminates everything around me for a split second, and I gasp when I see the face looking down at me, recognizing it immediately.

His arms tighten around me as he moves faster, branches and leaves smacking into us, his heavy footsteps splashing through the puddles as he runs.

"You can't save me," I mumble to him, my eyes so heavy I can't keep them open any longer.

"I'm getting you home."

He struggles to get the words out, his breathing labored from running so fast with me in his arms. He finally breaks free of the woods and races through the yard. He has no idea I'm not referring to what happened out here tonight. No idea I'm trying to warn him. He can save me from the darkness in the woods, but he'll never be able to save me from the darkness inside my soul.

"I'm sorry, I'm so sorry. I'll never let anything happen to you again."

Hugging my knees to my chest in the grass, I stare blankly at the cluster of trees and wooded area a few yards in front of me—the place where this nightmare in my mind began and never seems to end.

I try to let the anger flow through me and ease the pain I feel in my chest, but it's not working this time. I let my guard down, I let someone close, and this is my reward: more lies and more betrayal, just like always. Didn't I already learn my lesson by trying to be my parents' puppet, the good, perfect little daughter? I should have known better than to do the same with Nolan, trying to be a normal teenage girl with a normal, kind boy.

He's not kind. He's a liar, and I hate liars.

I hear a rustle in the trees to my left, someone pushing his way through the branches, leaves, and broken twigs on the ground. I see him emerge from the woods out of the corner of my eye, but I don't look until he's standing next to me, towering over me while I sit in the grass waiting.

He'll regret it, just like everyone else. He'll regret the lies and the betrayal and I'll make sure it hurts so he can understand what it's like to really feel pain.

"Sorry I'm late. I had some things to take care of at home," Nolan apologizes.

I finally turn my head and look up at him. The sun is behind him, creating darkness and shadows that blot out his features, just like that night in the woods. He turns his body and the sun finally lights up his face. I look up at him and *see* him, just like that night.

"You're a liar," I whisper angrily, pushing myself

up from the grass so I don't feel so small and power-less sitting beneath him.

His eyes narrow and he shakes his head in confu-sion.

"You didn't need to hear any gossip from the oth-er workers about what happened here that night, because you were *there*," I growl.

His eyes close, he lowers his head, and I can prac-tically feel the guilt seeping out of his pores.

"Ravenna, please let me explain," he says softly.

I ignore the pain in his voice and try not to think about how stupid I've been with him. How uncom-fortable it made me feel to have someone finally be nice to me, and care for me. He never cared for me; he's just like all the rest.

"You don't have to explain. You're a liar just like everyone else."

His pale blue eyes look at me with sadness and re-gret but I refuse to be weakened this time. I'm a fighter, and he's going to finally realize that.

"I'm sorry. Please, Ravenna, just let me—"

I cut off his anguished apology with a hard shove against his chest. He stumbles backward and I follow.

"Liar," I snarl through clenched teeth, smacking my palms as hard as I can into his chest again before he has a chance to get his footing from the first shove.

His feet tangle together and he starts to go down, but rights himself at the last second. I want him down, beneath me where he belongs, so I can climb on top of him, wrap my fingers around his neck and squeeze. *Squeeze* until he's clawing at my fingers and choking on his breath.

"RAVENNA, STOP!" he shouts, wrapping his hands around my wrists and pulling me roughly up against him.

I'm breathing heavily, the fire inside of me churning and growing, wanting to hurt him. Wanting to bring him pain so he knows what it feels like.

"I know you're angry, but you have to let me explain," he pleads. "I'm sorry I lied to you. You have no idea how sorry I am, but I had a reason. Please, just let me explain."

I force my anger down to a simmer since I'm still not ready to show him how truly strange I am, no matter how much I hate him right now.

"I know you don't trust me, but I need you to go somewhere with me," he explains quickly when he realizes I'm allowing him to continue. "I promise, if you just let me show you something, you'll understand why I did what I did."

He slowly drops my wrists, holding his hands up in surrender. "*Please,* just come with me."

Nolan turns and begins walking away from me, glancing over his shoulder with pleading eyes that urge me to follow. I grudgingly start walking a few feet behind him as he steps onto the overgrown path leading into the woods.

We walk in silence through the trees and memories of that dark, rainy night float through my mind, but still not enough for me to remember why I was running and whom I was running from.

After a few minutes, we emerge on the other side of the woods, stepping out onto another lawn that leads to a small white cottage a few hundred yards away. I pause, staring at the house that I didn't even know was here.

Nolan turns back to find me gaping, and he motions with his hands for me to keep following him. I let out an annoyed sigh, trailing behind him as he makes his way up to the front door of the house. He pauses with his hand on the knob, bowing his head and closing his eyes.

"I never lied when I told you I care about you, Ravenna. I do, I promise. You have no idea how much it's been killing me keeping this from you, but I had to do it."

"What is this place?"

He turns back to look at me and shrugs. "It's my home. Well, my parents' home. We've lived here all my life. Before my father died, he used to be the head groundskeeper at the prison and this house came with the job. It's one of the reasons I wasn't completely honest with you."

Nolan looks away and opens the door, stepping inside the small house. I follow behind him, moving into a tiny living room, shrouded in darkness with the shades drawn.

"What's the other reason?" I ask as he moves around me to close the door behind us.

I hear a cough and a gentle groan of pain in the far corner of the room. I take a step toward the noise, squinting my eyes as I realize there's someone sitting in a chair in the shadows.

Nolan moves up behind me, his chest pressing against my shoulder as he looks in the same direction.

"She's the other reason," he whispers, moving around me to walk farther into the room and over to the corner.

I watch silently as he raises one of the window shades a few inches to let some sunlight filter in, the bright rays shining down on the lower half of the woman in the chair, who's sitting up with a blanket draped over her lap. Nolan squats down in front of her, placing his hands on her knees.

"Mom, I brought company with me," he tells her with a smile, looking back over his shoulder at me. "Ravenna, this is my mother, Beatrice Michaels."

My feet inch across the carpet as my eyes take in the frail, sickly woman staring at me. Her dressing gown looks two sizes too big for her small body, but I can still see the bones of her shoulders sticking up through the material. Her face is sunken in and pale, and the turban-style wrap on her head doesn't fully hide the fact that she doesn't have any hair.

Nolan watches me as I look at her, his quiet voice filling the room. "She has cancer and it's progressed pretty rapidly in the last few years. But she's a fighter, and she's going to get better real soon."

"Don't talk about me like I'm not here, son," Beatrice mumbles, her body wracked with a coughing fit.

Nolan reaches between her blanket-covered leg and the arm of the chair, pulling out a handkerchief and handing it to her. Beatrice quickly grabs it, holding the white cloth against her mouth as she coughs. When she lowers her hand from her mouth, I notice the handkerchief is dotted in bright red blood.

"So you came back," Beatrice says as she looks me up and down while I stand like a statue in the middle of the living room. "I always knew you'd come back and finish what you started."

Nolan stands up next to her chair and looks between us. "Mom, what are you talking about? Ravenna has never been here before."

Beatrice shakes her head slowly back and forth, her eyes never leaving mine. "I warned them, but they didn't listen. Now they're surrounded by death."

Nolan puts his hand on her frail shoulder, rubbing it gently. "Why don't you take a nap? When you wake up, it will be time for your medicine again."

He leans down and places a kiss on the papery skin of her cheek, walking back to me. Grabbing my hand, he laces his fingers through mine, gently tugging me toward the door. I let him hold my hand and lead me away, only because I don't like the way his mother is staring at me. My skin crawls with each word she speaks, and I just want to get as far away from her as possible.

"The dead speak, and you should always listen," Beatrice shouts in between coughs as Nolan opens the front door. "I see the letter *T*. Do you remember? Do you know? *T* means death, death means *T*. Remember *T*. REMEMBER! My husband pulled that little body from the water. He was a hero and he paid with his life for going against evil's wishes."

Nolan quickly pulls me the rest of the way out the door, closing it gently behind us. I feel sweat trickling down my back and a sharp pain shoots through my head, stabbing behind my eyes and making me squeeze them tightly closed. I let Nolan blindly lead me down the stairs and back into the woods, moving us quickly through the path until we come out on the other side on the prison grounds. He pauses in the middle of the yard, and I finally open my eyes as the headache subsides. He faces me, and I stare up at him silently while he rubs his hands up and down my arms soothingly.

"I'm sorry about that. The medication she's on sometimes makes her say some pretty strange things," he explains. "Before my father died, she used to work at the prison doing palm readings for some of the tour groups. She's always had kind of a sixth sense about things and your father thought it would be something fun to add to the tours. Mostly, it's a lot of just reading people and their reactions, telling them things you know will get a rise out of them. It's not like she actually speaks to the dead or anything."

Nolan laughs uncomfortably, but I look away from him and stare at the prison off in the distance, thinking about the words she spoke to me. He continues talking to fill the awkward silence.

"I heard shouts and screaming coming from the woods that night. I had woken to give my mother her medicine," he explains, his hands still moving softly up and down my arms while he speaks. "I ran into the woods and found you lying there on the ground, bleeding from the head. I scooped you up and took you back to the prison. Your father told me to put you on the floor and leave immediately. When I tried to argue with him about calling the police or getting you to a hospital, he threatened my job. He told me if I said one word about anything, he'd fire me and kick my mother and I out of the house."

Swinging my gaze away from the prison, I look up at him, seeing the truth written all over his face: the truth, the guilt, the pain, and the remorse.

"Your father only gave me this job because he felt bad that my father had a heart attack here on the prison grounds while he was working. If I lose this job, I'll have no way to pay for my mother's medication, and we'll have nowhere to live. I couldn't risk that, Ravenna, I just couldn't. My mother is all I have left," he finishes, a slight quiver of emotion filling his voice.

"It's fine, Nolan, I get it," I tell him, resolving him of some of his guilt. Even if I don't understand the kind of love and affection he has toward his mother, I'm not so cold and dead inside that I can't see he had no other choice. If my father found out he shared this with me, he'd toss them both out onto the street without giving it a second thought. He doesn't care who he hurts, as long as his secrets are safe.

T means death, death means T. Remember T. RE-MEMBER!

"It's not fine, Ravenna. I should have told you. If I thought that information would help you figure things out, I would have, I promise. You already know your father has problems, and he's keeping things from you. Telling you he threatened my job and my family's home wouldn't have done anything but make your father follow through with his threat and I just couldn't chance it," Nolan finishes.

"So your father worked here before you did?" I ask, changing the subject before I start to enjoy having his hands on me.

His hands drop from my arms as I move away, but I give him a smile so he doesn't think I'm mad at what he told me.

"Yes, he got the job when I was a couple years old," Nolan confirms, walking with me back to the prison.

T means death, death means T. Remember T. RE-

MEMBER!

"Your mom said something about pulling a little body out of the water. Do you think she meant the accident in the lake when I was little? Was your dad the one who rescued me?"

Nolan shrugs. "It could be true, but I have no idea. Sometimes the things she says make sense, and other times she's extremely confused, mixing up things that happened in her life with things she read in the newspaper or heard on the news. I never heard either one of them talk about you falling in the lake when you were little and my father pulling you out, so it could just have been her mind playing tricks on her."

T means death, death means T. Remember T. RE-MEMBER!

I don't remember meeting Nolan's father when I was little, but that doesn't mean anything since I don't remember much of my childhood.

With another promise to Nolan that I'm not angry that he kept this secret from me, I leave him to go back home to tend to his mother while I head upstairs to figure out a way to force my father out of his office.

"My name is Ravenna Duskin. I'm eighteen years old, I live in a prison, and I have no idea why the letter *T* fills me with dread."

CHAPTER 16

"**T** MEANS DEATH, death means T," I say to myself softly, writing the words on the back of an old grocery list my mother left pinned to the front of the fridge.

Underlining what I just wrote, I set the pencil down on the kitchen table and lean back in my chair to stare at the words. I have no idea why I'm trying to figure out if the ramblings of a sick, dying woman mean something, but I'm out of options right now. I can't get the image of her eyes out of my head. They weren't in a daze or clouded over like someone on the verge of death, pumped full of so much medication that they weren't aware of anything. Beatrice's eyes were bright and clear, and they never strayed from my face. I don't care if Nolan thinks her palm reading was just an exaggeration of a sixth sense she has or that she sometimes confuses things she's seen or heard with real life. The words she spoke made the hair on my arms stand up and made me want to run from the room so she'd stop talking. As much as I hated it, I couldn't ignore it. If I hadn't trusted my instincts recently, I'd still assume my mind was playing tricks on me and I couldn't swim. If I'd ignored my gut feelings, I'd still be dressing the way my parents demanded and braiding my hair every morning. I never would have found that suitcase full of clothes I knew were mine, and I never would have remembered being in that spare bedroom before.

Nolan's mother might have given me another piece of the puzzle, no matter how weird and confusing it was. Her words didn't evoke any memories, but they still left me feeling uneasy and—I hate to say it—afraid. Fear is for the weak, and I will never be weak again.

"T means death, death means T," I say out loud again, hoping it will trigger something. Obviously the letter T stands for something. Picking up the pencil again, I start writing names I know that begin with T.

Tanner Duskin, my father

Trudy, now my ex-best friend

There's only one more person I know whose name begins with the letter T and my hand starts to shake when I merely think his name. I hear a loud *snap* and realize I just broke the pencil in half from squeezing it so hard. Closing my eyes and taking a few deep breaths, I drop the eraser end of the pencil and use the small broken tip to write the last name.

Dr. Raymond Thomas…

I put an ellipsis after his name because I have no

idea who he is to me. I only know that his name fills me with dread, makes my skin crawl, and fills me with the urge to scream at the top of my lungs until my throat is raw.

I've avoided thinking about him since the night my mother shot herself. When I asked her about him, she said something about how he only did what they asked him to do. I'm assuming she meant her and my father, but who knows? She might not have even been talking about the doctor. For all I know, she hadn't even heard me say his name and was rambling about something else.

I can't avoid it any longer. I have to think about him, even if my mind is screaming at me to run away because it will do nothing but hurt me. There has to be a reason why just the mention of his name by Dr. Beall caused me to black out on the stairs. There has to be a plausible explanation for why the few times his name has quickly flown through my mind by accident since then, I feel like someone is physically causing me pain, and I have to stop, remember to breathe, and calm down.

When I heard his name, it was almost as if he became one with my most painful memories and the scariest dreams I've had since this all began. Even if I know it's something I have to remember to put all of this missing information in my mind together once and for all, it's still something I've been refusing to do since that night.

Those memories make me feel so much more than the comfort of hate and anger. They make me want to do more than just fantasize about harming people. It's one thing to think about these things and realize there might be something just a little bit strange about myself. It's a whole other nightmare to feel so over-whelmed by those feelings—by the mere thought of one man—that I know without a shadow of a doubt that I could end someone's life and not feel bad about it at all.

I'm not a killer. I don't know much, but at least I know that.

Right when I come to terms with it, forcing my-self to think about that man just to see if I can remember *something* about the person who elicits so much pain inside me, I hear the door to my father's office fly open, slamming against the opposite wall.

Pushing the chair away from the table, I get up and hurriedly go to the kitchen doorway to see my father head toward the stairs.

"We're out of whiskey. I can't believe Claudia hasn't bought more. I'll have to speak to her about it," my father mumbles as he stomps down the stairs, the keys to his car jangling in his hand.

I was fully prepared to bang on his door later to demand he come out and talk to me. I figured I had nothing to lose by telling him I've started remember-ing things, just to see what he would say, even though I'm pretty positive he would just continue lying. He seems to be an expert at that. I want him to know that I'm aware that he lied to both Dr. Beall and me when he said he didn't know how I got back to the prison after getting hurt that night. I want to be looking him in the eye when he realizes that I know all about the threats he made to Nolan, and I want to see his reaction when I mention the name of Dr. Thomas.

Hearing him speak to himself about my mother like she's still alive immediately kills that plan. I should probably stop him from driving anywhere in his condition, but at this point I don't really care if he crashes his car and hurts himself, or even if he gets himself killed. He's avoided me for days, the first time he even looked at me being the night my mother killed herself, and he shouted accusations and blame at me. He quickly laid waste to the silly notions I had when I first woke up after the accident, that he was a good father and truly loved me. I shouldn't have ignored my instincts that day in the cell block, when it felt foreign to hug him, as if I'd never done it before. I shouldn't have brushed aside the gut feelings I had that he was lying to me from day one. Maybe if I had listened to what my head was telling me sooner, I'd have remembered everything by now.

Even though one of my plans has to be put on hold for now, I quickly realize another door just opened for me. Literally. My father's office door is wide open and when I hear the faint rumble of his car starting outside, followed by the peeling of tires on the driveway, I race across the living room.

The room reeks of stale liquor, sweat, and vomit, and nothing like the pipe smoke and peppermint that usually surrounds him. I pull the neck of my shirt up over my nose, masking some of the smell before I get sick, as I move farther into the room.

I immediately spot the back of a framed photo on the corner of his desk, grabbing it and turning it around to inspect it. Contrary to what my mother said, the photo doesn't tell me any secrets. It doesn't even conjure up any memories as I stare at it. Even though it was taken on the main stairway leading up to this area, it seems to have been taken by a professional photographer, since the name of the studio is embossed on the picture in the bottom right-hand corner. There's nothing special about the photo; it's a typical family photo with my father sitting on one step and my mother on the one right below him, her body turned to the side with her knees demurely pressed together. I would guess I'm around five or so, and I'm seated right next to my mother with one elbow casually resting on her legs and the other in my lap, and she has her arm around my back, part of her hand that holds onto my hip visible.

The only thing that is strange and a little telling is that my father seems to be separated from us. He doesn't have his hand on her shoulder, he's not reaching down to lovingly touch me in any way, and he's the only one not smiling, his frown lines deep and prominent. Even though both of our smiles—my mother's and mine—seem a tad forced, at least we don't look ticked off at the world. He stares into the camera as if at any moment he's going to jump up and start yelling at everyone. Looking closer at the space between my mother and me, I can see he has his hands clenched into fists, one on each knee.

Shaking my head, I wonder why they even went through with this photo. My father doesn't seem like the type of person who can be coerced into anything, but it's kind of obvious he was pushed into taking this picture when he clearly wasn't having a good day.

I'm not sure if this is what my mother meant when she said the photo would tell me the truth. I already figured out my father isn't very good at disguising his anger, even in a family photograph. I'm guessing I'm around five in the photo and that was the year the whole lake incident happened. Maybe that's what my mother was talking about and the cause for the mad look on my father's face. Maybe this was taken around that same time or even the same day.

I quickly dismiss that notion, though, placing the photo back where it was. The accident when I was five is the one thing they didn't keep from me and pretty much the only thing they were quick to talk about when I asked. It's not a secret or a truth that I needed to figure out.

Moving around behind my father's desk, I wonder if her mention of the photo was just a confusing way to point me in the right direction. I sit down in my father's chair and begin pulling open drawers. For the next few minutes, I flip through every piece of paper in each drawer, finding nothing but financial paperwork about the prison, old blueprints, and other miscellaneous items that are useless to me. In frustration, I slam the last drawer closed so forcefully that it shakes the desk, knocking our family photo off the corner of the desk and onto the floor.

Getting up from the chair, I walk to the front of the desk to pick up the photo, thankful that my father has a small area rug under his desk that prevented the glass in the frame from shattering. That would've made it a little harder to cover my tracks so he wouldn't know I was in here. Considering his drunken behavior, I doubt he'd even notice, but I'm not taking any chances. The less he knows about how suspicious I am of him, the better.

Lifting the frame from the rug, the cardboard backing falls off, and with it, a small slip of folded paper. Setting the frame to the side, I pick up the paper, unfolding it to find a three-digit code written in the bottom left-hand corner. Looking around the room again, I ponder what the code is for and why my father would have it hidden in such a strange place. Rising to my feet with the paper in my hand, I stand in the middle of the office, my eyes panning the room. I glance at the bookshelf on one wall, filled with encyclopedias, literary classics, and a few random objects like a coffee cup holding paperclips, a flashlight, and one empty bottle of whiskey that somehow didn't make it outside with the rest he finished. Slowly, I turn in a circle, looking at all the old photographs in large ornate frames that hang on the walls. They are all black and white, and each one is of the prison at various times through the years. A few were taken on the outside and the rest were taken inside when the prison was still functioning, showing inmates eating in the mess hall, working out in the fields, or lined up waiting for the showers.

My eyes are quickly scanning the photos since they are all pretty much the same, when something jumps out at me and I look back, realizing I inadvertently skipped over one photo that is not like the others.

I move closer and stand right in front of it. It's a picture of this very room, and my eyes must have skipped over it because it's black and white like all the rest and even the same size as the others. I'm not sure when it was taken, but I'm assuming it's from before we moved in, since the walls in the photo are completely bare and the room is empty of any furniture. The only thing in the room is a safe, built into the wall where I currently stand. Putting the slip of paper between my teeth, I grab onto the frame of the picture and lift it off of its hook. My heartbeat picks up with excitement as soon as I see the safe hiding right behind the photo. Leaning the picture against the wall at my feet, I rip the paper from my mouth and reread the numbers. Holding my breath, I turn the dial on the combination lock in the same order as written on the paper.

Right thirteen, left twenty-four, right seven.

As soon as the arrow on the dial points to the number seven, I hear a soft click and the door to the safe pops open. Letting the paper in my hand flutter to the ground, I quickly open the door all the way, a little shocked that inside such a large safe is only one single manila folder, barely visible because it's so flat and obviously not filled with too many papers.

Even though I expected this thing to be packed full of items, I know immediately that I found what I was looking for and that my mother actually told me something important, even if it was a riddle I had to figure out.

Sliding the thin folder out of the safe, I turn around and sit down on the floor right below it, pausing for a moment to listen for any noises indicating my father has returned. When I hear nothing but silence, I look down at the folder and see our last name printed on the tab from a typewriter.

Flipping it open, I see the words *Gallow's Hill Inmate Transfer Request* printed at the top, and right beneath that on the very first line, the prisoner's name is listed as Tobias Duskin. I try to remember if I've ever heard that name before, but I draw a blank, which doesn't surprise me. Still I huff out an irritated breath.

I rapidly scan the page, stopping when I get to the box that lists the prisoner's next of kin, my mouth dropping open in shock.

Margarita Duskin, mother, deceased.

Dimitri Duskin, father, deceased.

Tanner Duskin, brother.

Tobias Duskin was my father's brother and my uncle, older than him by two years, according to his birthdate listed on the form. Why don't I remember my parents ever mentioning the existence of an uncle? As far as I know, we don't have any living relatives, my parents supposedly both being only children, and their parents passing on before I was born. At least they didn't lie about the death of my grandparents, according to this paperwork, but why would they never tell me that I had an uncle? Butterflies flap around in my stomach when it occurs to me that I have an uncle whose name begins with the letter T. The letter that Beatrice was so adamant I remember and one more person to add to my list, even though I didn't even realize he existed until just now.

Flipping through the few pages in the file, I find a couple of handwritten reports from doctors, guards, and the wardens before my father's time, quickly understanding why my parents thought it was best to keep Tobias Duskin's identity a secret, even if my mother felt the need to cryptically point me in the direction of this file right before she died. I'm not going to lie. Reading about this long-lost uncle, I suddenly feel like the disturbing thoughts I have and the urges I fantasize about in order to feel exhilarated and alive make a little more sense now, and I might have just found a reason for my behavior. It appears this type of thing runs in the family, although my uncle seems to have taken his urges to the next level, while I make sure mine remain only in my head.

Arrested at the age of eighteen for the brutal slaying of both his parents with a hammer while they slept peacefully in their beds, then going on to murder three more innocent bystanders on his way out of town, Tobias Duskin confessed to the murders and was immediately sentenced to life in prison. He wasn't exactly a model prisoner, according to his record, constantly starting fights and spending the majority of his time in solitary confinement, even killing three other prisoners while he was in here.

When this placed closed a few years after I was born, all 1,900 prisoners were bused to various prisons, some to the new one built just an hour away from here, and others to ones in bordering states. Assuming my uncle was moved with everyone else when the doors closed, I get to the final page of the file that lists the date of his transfer and start to get an uneasy feeling as I think about everything I've learned so far about myself, my life, and that of my parents and their behavior with me and with each other.

I think about the things my mother rambled about, her sins and weaknesses, and how she made a mistake, and everyone suffered because of it. One of the things she said sticks out in my mind, and I can hear her pained voice in my head as she pleaded with me.

"You need to find him. You need to talk to him. You'll see him, and you'll understand. It will all make sense then."

I've been assuming she was referring to Dr. Thomas. It's the only thing that made sense since she went off the deep end only hours after Dr. Beall told me about him.

Everything clicks together in my mind, and I'm surprised it never occurred to me before now. The distance between my father and I, and the feelings I've had that he's never really loved me and even seems to hate the very sight of me. How I don't remember a happy childhood and all of the sweet family photos that look fake and forced. Memories of being somewhere other than here, filled with misery and pain, and the suitcase in the spare bedroom filled with my clothes. The dreams and memories of staying in that room and at some point, coming back and being reminded by Ike of the rules around the house, like I was a guest.

I'm pretty sure this file proves there's a reason my father doesn't like me and a reason for my parents' strained relationship, probably going on for much longer than after my accident. Most likely for eighteen years.

Dated exactly nine months before I was born, I reread the reason for the transfer request written in my father's handwriting, read it out loud in the quiet room, just so I can hear myself say it to make sure it's real and I'm not seeing things.

"I, Tanner Duskin, warden of Gallow's Hill, hereby request a transfer of prisoner A45295, Tobias A. Duskin, for bribing and threatening two Gallow's Hill guards in order to receive special treatment of unauthorized time away from his cell, occurring during nighttime lockdown several times a month and continuing for six months. During this time, Tobias Duskin privately met with Mrs. Claudia Duskin."

Putting the paper back inside the file, I push myself up from the floor and slide it back into the safe, closing the door and spinning the dial to lock it.

I hear my father's rusty brakes screech to a stop outside, and take one last look around the office to make sure everything is how he left it and then quickly exit the room, locking myself inside the spare bedroom. Leaning my back against the door, I listen as my father pounds up the stairs, goes into his office, and slams the door closed.

"My name is Ravenna Duskin. I'm eighteen years old, I live in a prison, and I think I just found out who my real father is."

CHAPTER 17

"JESUS, RAVENNA, HOW are you not completely breaking down right now?" Nolan asks as we stand behind the counter in the souvenir room.

I really wanted to make him suffer more and ignore him for a few more days for not telling me he was the one who carried me out of the woods, but it's not very easy trying to solve a mystery all by myself when my mind is keeping so much information from me, and the things I *do* figure out just create more questions. Also, it's so pathetic that he continues coming back here to be with me, considering I'm not exactly the most enjoyable person to be around, that I have no choice but to feel sorry for him. How miserable is his life that he spent two years pining for me when I was nothing but a complete snob who wouldn't even look in his direction? And now that I am paying him attention, it mostly involves constantly making him stop touching me or keeping him at a distance so he doesn't even think about touching me. Then there's the whole figuring out things about me that are getting increasingly worse, making it more than obvious he should probably get far away from me as quickly as possible.

His mother seriously needs to die soon so he can finally stop hovering over her, get out of that house, and see that there are much better options than me out there. For now, I guess I'll just be content with the fact that he *does* keep coming back, since he's the only confidant I have. Now that he no longer feels guilty every time he's around me and doesn't have to avoid my questions about that night in the woods, he never seems to stop talking, eager to help me try and figure out the rest of the mysteries I can't fully remember yet.

"What's the point in breaking down?" I ask, replying to his question. "I've already lost my mind so having a breakdown would just be repetitive."

My voice is filled with sarcasm as I flip the pages of the book in front of me a little too forcefully, accidentally ripping one in half. Luckily it isn't one I need.

"You haven't lost your mind," he reassures me. "It's obvious you were right to question the things your parents were trying to make you believe, even though we have no clue what the point of all those lies were when they knew you were going to start remembering things eventually."

Yet another thing I've been obsessing about for entirely too many hours of every day. Dr. Beall told me and my parents multiple times that my memory loss wasn't permanent. Why in the world did they think I'd never figure out they were lying to me? YEAH, WHY DIDN'T THEY? LOL.

"They definitely had secrets," Nolan continues. "I'm just having a hard time believing that your proper, always put together mother had an affair with a prisoner. Especially a convicted killer who bludgeoned his own parents and three strangers to death with a hammer…and who just so happened to be her husband's older brother. Not only is that the craziest thing I've ever heard, she did this right under her husband's nose, in the prison he ran, where at any time someone who worked here could have ratted them out."

I sigh, continuing to flip through the telephone directory until I get to the S's.

"Well, it's not like there was a piece of paper in the file that came right out and said Tobias is my father, but it seems a little obvious, considering he was secretly meeting with my mother for months and my father requested his transfer nine months before I was born," I tell him, running my finger down the page.

"How was this guy even allowed to be here at Gallow's Hill when his brother was the warden?" Nolan asks.

"There was another sheet of paper in the file that had a list of special rules and regulations the state made my father agree to in order to allow Tobias to stay here while my father was the warden," I tell him distractedly as I flip to the next page and keep looking down the list. "Stuff like twice as many prison visits from the state to interview guards and other employees to make sure my father wasn't giving Tobias special treatment and additional reports to fill out that had to be signed by everyone who came in contact with Tobias. I'm assuming the state knew it would only be a matter of time before they shut down the prison and letting Tobias stay here wasn't that big of a deal in the grand scheme of things."

Nolan leans close to look over my shoulder and I try not to move away. Now that I've decided to forgive him for the time being, I'm right back to being irritated that having him touch me or try to get close to me puts me on edge. I hate it just as much as I love it and I really don't need this nonsense right now, but I do need the use of his brain since it seems to be in much better working order than mine. The only reason I'm searching through the phone book right now is because of his suggestion.

"All of this is just so weird because in the two years I've worked here, I've never seen your father be anything but nice to you whenever you two were outside together," Nolan muses quietly, right by my ear. "I just don't understand why all of a sudden you don't get along, and he's acting completely different with you."

I clench my teeth and try not to rip out a handful of pages from the phone book, crumple them in a wadded-up ball, and shove them right in his mouth.

"We don't get along because I've caught him in lies, and he screamed at me and told me it was my fault my mother killed herself," I reply in a snippy voice.

Nolan puts his hand on my back and pats me softly, and I force myself not to think about finding the nearest sharp object and chopping off his hand.

"Hey, I'm sorry, don't be mad. I'm not saying it's not true. I'm just talking out loud, trying to figure things out," he apologizes. "I'll admit I wasn't sure at first about your theory that everything revolves around the night I found you in the woods, but there has to be a reason it's one of the only things you still can't remember and why everything around this place seems to be imploding since that night."

I nod, dismissing my thoughts of the bloody stump of his hand thumping onto the porch steps—for now.

"When I first woke up, Dr. Beall told me that sometimes our mind puts traumatic events into a secret corner until we're ready to process them, and I just had to give it time, be patient, and I would eventually remember everything. Considering the things I've already remembered and how awful *they* are, I'm assuming this must be really bad."

Nolan starts moving his hand in a slow, small circle in the middle of my back, and I try to enjoy it like a regular eighteen-year-old girl would if a cute older boy showed affection and comforted her. It does feel nice physically; it just doesn't comfort me mentally.

"I hate that everything seems to keep snowballing ever since that night. And I hate myself for being just the tiniest bit happy that the destruction of your life might be the only reason you acknowledged my existence in two years," he admits.

I stop searching through the phone book to look at him questioningly.

"I thought you said I started acting differently and began talking to you right before that night?"

He shrugs. "You did, but it felt fake for some reason. Nothing at all like it has been the last few weeks. I mean, something about the different way you dressed and the way you wore your hair the first couple of times you spoke to me felt like it actually matched your personality, but I don't know. It was just weird how it happened so out of the blue, and even though I liked it that you were finally talking to me, it never felt genuine."

I look back down at the phone book before I start comparing his blue eyes to oceans or the sky or something else that only stupid girls do.

"So what you're saying is that all it took was a huge, bloody gash in my forehead and a little memory loss to make me a more honest person?" I ask.

"As horrible as that sounds, yes," Nolan agrees.

I swallow back the need to laugh long and hard. Just moments ago I daydreamed about slicing off his hand, all the while pretending I wasn't bothered by his touching me. It makes me want to roll my eyes that he's so clueless.

"I just want to help you get to the bottom of this, so you can stop feeling so angry and finally be able to move on," he tells me.

If only it were that simple. Poor, clueless Nolan.

"Aha! Found it," I announce, my finger underneath the name I've been searching for. "Strongfield Penitentiary."

This prison is the fourth one out of five listed on the papers I found in my father's safe for potential institutions Tobias could be relocated to. Nolan suggested I start calling the prisons to see if he's currently an inmate at any of them. The first three informed me that they didn't have an inmate by that name, nor had they ever in the past.

Picking up the phone on the counter, I turn the dial while Nolan rattles off the numbers for me. Someone picks up after the first ring and I explain once again that I'm looking for a relative by the name of Tobias Duskin. I'm losing a little hope at this point, though. He might not even be alive anymore, let alone housed in the only other prison within easy driving distance from here.

The woman puts me on hold and it only takes a few minutes for her to come back on the line. "Yes, we do have a man here by the name of Tobias Duskin. He's been here since he was transferred in

1947."

"Don't you mean 1946?" I ask, knowing the date of the transfer request on the form I saw was exactly nine months before I was born and the whole reason I put everything together. Maybe that was some sort of weird, coincidental mistake, and my father wrote the wrong date. Maybe I jumped to conclusions because that answer made so many things fall into place and gave them an explanation, instead of jumbled nonsense in my head. Her private nightly meetings might not have been definitive proof of an affair, maybe it was just…I don't know, family stuff. Stranger things have happened, especially recently. It's not like I found a birth certificate in the file listing Tobias as my father.

The woman tells me to hold again and I hear her shuffling through papers. After a few minutes, she comes back on the line. "No, it was definitely 1947, although we did receive the first request in 1946. Unfortunately, we were full at that time and couldn't accommodate the request. It says here that on September 3, 1947, we received a phone call from his previous place of incarceration, Gallow's Hill. It doesn't give much of an explanation on the paperwork I have access to; it just says an emergency call was placed requesting transfer immediately because of a dangerous, possibly life-threatening event that Gallow's Hill was unable to handle. He was picked up by us that same day."

I barely pay attention to what she says after she informed me of his official transfer date, and when she rattles off visitation days and hours, at least I snap to it long enough to scribble those down on the sales ledger next to the phone that's open to a blank page. When she asks me if I need anything else, I don't bother answering her; I just hang up the phone.

"I'm guessing by what I heard you found the right prison. Did he die or something? Is that why you look like you're in shock?" Nolan asks, pulling the ledger across the counter toward him to see what I wrote down.

"He's still alive and yes, he's there. Tobias wasn't transferred nine months before I was born like I thought," I mumble, going through the woman's words in my head again, realizing I was right all along with my suspicions, and I feel even more sure of them now than I was five minutes ago.

"Okay, so what does that mean? You don't think he's your father now? It was all just suspicion anyway so it's not like we had any concrete proof," he reminds me, pushing the ledger back where it was.

"I think we have even better proof now," I inform him, ripping the page out of the ledger with the visitation times. "He wasn't transferred in 1946, but an immediate and emergency transfer was called in to Strongfield on the same day I was born. That seems a little bit strange to me. How about you?"

Nolan runs his hand through his hair and shakes

his head back and forth slowly. "Yeah, that's a little too coincidental even for me. I'm assuming you'd like to go on a little road trip, since Strongfield is only an hour away, and if the times on the paper in your hand are visiting hours, that means we still have five hours left today."

Turning away from the counter, I grab the spare set of my father's car keys from the hook hanging on the wall. Thankfully, I don't need to wait for another random bit of luck that my father will emerge from his office, allowing me the opportunity to steal his car keys that are always kept in his desk—or be forced to have Nolan pick the lock and try to come up with a lie about why I need the keys.

Feeling an abnormal burst of happiness and, strangely, not at all uncomfortable with it, I decide to try my hand at being just a little bit nice, tossing the keys to Nolan and informing him that he can drive. It's the only bit of control I feel comfortable conceding to right now.

When we walk out the front door, I make sure the "Closed Indefinitely" sign is still hanging right in the middle of it. I put it there the first day my father locked himself away and refused to deal with anything, including the running of this prison. After one hour of dealing with annoying, nosy tourists, I wrote the words in big, bold letters and taped the sign prominently to the door. I'm not sure what will happen if the state finds out how long my father has been ignoring the business, since this is a historical building and they fund everything, as well as give us a place to live free of charge. Frankly, I don't really care.

After I woke up from my accident, every morning my mother would braid my hair, and repeatedly tell me all the facts about the girl I supposedly was, but there was only one I liked to hear: I had a full scholarship waiting for me at a very nice college a few hours away, and that scholarship included room and board, as well as all of my meals. Even if I never figure everything out or regain all of my memories, at least I'll be able to get the hell away from this place that seems to be the root of everything that has gone wrong in my life, leave my father far behind, and never look back ever again.

Nolan opens the passenger door of my father's car like the perfect gentleman he is, closing it when he's sure I'm all the way inside. I watch as he walks around the front of the vehicle and I whisper my mantra that is constantly evolving.

"My name is Ravenna Duskin. I'm eighteen years old, I live in a prison, and I'm going to meet my real father."

CHAPTER 18

I TRIED TO spend the hour-long car ride to Strong-field State Penitentiary in silence, so I could plan what I would say to Tobias Duskin, but Nolan wanted to talk, as usual. Since I couldn't force him to shut up by grabbing the steering wheel and swerving us into a tree without injuring myself as well, I gave up my desire for quiet time so we could go over the list of things I knew versus things that were still questionable.

"Okay, the first thing that felt off to you was the way you wore your hair and the clothes in your closet, both of which your mother insisted were your style and your daily uniform, correct?" Nolan asks as I look out the window watching the scenery fly by.

"Correct," I reply. "Both of those things felt completely wrong the very first day I woke up after the accident."

Nolan nods, flipping on the wipers when a few drops of rain splatter against the windshield. "You felt better when you took a pair of scissors to your clothes and let down your hair, and we found an entire suitcase of clothes that you somehow knew were yours."

"Yes," I quickly answer, turning my head to look at his profile. "But even though I feel more like myself now, you confirmed what my mother told me about my clothes and hair—that the entire two years you worked at the prison, excluding the few days leading up to my night in the woods, I did in fact always wear those ugly dresses with tightly braided hair. So that's still a little weird."

Nolan shrugs as he concentrates on the road in front of us when the rain picks up. "Still, you had dreams and a few flashes of memory about you looking different and about the suitcase of clothes. So for right now, we're going to put that in the positive column and consider it a memory successfully retrieved."

We continued going back and forth, having plenty of time to rehash everything. The drive took longer than expected due to the summer shower turning into a downpour, making it harder to see while driving.

In the memories retrieved column I have:

− Feeling uncomfortable with my father's affection, almost as if he'd never shown me any before. That affection quickly turned into his avoidance and then downright hostility toward me. I might not have confirmed with one-hundred-percent certainty that the cause for all of this is that he's not my father, but it's going into the positive column for now.

− The feelings of hatred toward Trudy, my supposed best friend, as well as memories of the two of us fighting, and the suspicious scratches on her neck that I knew she was lying about. This was confirmed as something real and part of my missing memories when I finally remembered our entire fight and confronted her about it. Being stuck in a small, confined space and forced to talk to Nolan this entire trip suddenly became enjoyable when I got to stare at his profile as I relived all of this for him. I got to witness his face turn a bright shade of red, followed by repeated apologies, and pathetic begging, ending with pitiful assurances that Trudy kissed him, not the other way around, and he made it clear to her that he didn't like her that way.

– Nolan not liking me very much, as well as my feeling uneasy around him, was finally figured out when I remembered he was with me in the woods, that he was the one who found me and took me home, then proceeded to lie about it. I decide to keep him in the dark about how none of this has fixed my anxiety around him—his affection is foreign to me—and that I calm my feelings of discomfort by imagining cutting off his limbs. I mean, he's nice and he's helping me, so that seems like a conversation better left for never.

At this point, the only things in the negative column that I still can't remember fully or explain at all would be the horrible memories and dreams about pain and misery, all surrounding Dr. Thomas, and, of course, what forced me that night to run away from the prison and out into the woods. Nolan is adamant that anything his mother said during our short visit should go in this column as well, since the medication she's on confuses her mind, but I'm still secretly placing her mention of the letter T somewhere in between the two lists. There has to be a reason I felt it was important and that she knew a truth about me I couldn't quite figure out. I wanted her to stop talking because her words made my skin crawl and that's not something I can easily push aside. The things I'm most uncomfortable with seem to keep turning into true facts about my life.

As soon as we finish with our list, Nolan is turning on his blinker and pulling into the parking lot of Strongfield.

"A lot different from Gallow's Hill, isn't it?" he asks as he finds a parking space in the visitor's lot and turns off the engine.

I don't answer him as I lean closer to the dash to stare at the building in front of us. It's obviously quite different than Gallow's Hill since it was built in the early 1940's as opposed to the 1800's. It's more modern and simple—just one long, single-story building surrounded by a chain-link fence.

"This place was built specifically for overflow when Gallow's Hill became too crowded," I tell him. "Then when we closed, the majority of our prisoners were relocated here. With all of the new prisoners' rights laws enacted since Gallow's Hill closed, they definitely have better accommodations and less risk of guards feeling like they could treat them however they wished."

Nolan and I exit the car, and he slides his hand into mine as we take off running through the rain, soon making it to the covered sidewalk that leads to the visitor's entrance on the side of the building. My palms are sweating, and I can't stop the slight tremor that travels through my arms as we shake the rain from our hair and clothing. Nolan pulls the hand he's holding up to his chest, pressing it against his heart.

"Don't be nervous. I'll be right there next to you," he assures me.

I keep my mouth shut as he opens the door, drops my hand, and gestures for me to go inside ahead of him. I'm not nervous about seeing Tobias because I know it will provide answers to my questions. His handholding and overall niceness is what make me nervous and want to run away screaming.

Nolan tries to take my hand again, but I yank it away, moving farther ahead of him and straight to the check-in counter, where a grandmotherly woman sits with a notebook and pen in front of her.

She turns the notebook around, pushing it across the counter toward me with a smile on her face. "Just print your name and the name of the prisoner you'll be visiting today."

Grabbing the pen from the top of the book, I neatly print my information at the bottom of the other list of sign-ins. When I'm finished, she turns the book around, glances quickly at what I wrote and begins to get up from her chair. She pauses halfway out of her seat, her head whipping back down to the book. She lifts it from the counter and pulls it closer to her face, her eyes widening as she looks back and forth between me and the book.

"Tobias Duskin? You're here to visit Tobias Duskin?" she asks in a quiet, shocked voice.

"Yes, is that a problem?"

I start to worry that maybe we made the trip out here for no reason. Maybe he's not allowed to have visitors. Considering the extent of his crimes, I probably should have thought about that before jumping into the car and racing over here, but the only thing on my mind was getting answers that only he could provide.

"No, no problem," she replies, the smile again on her face as she places the book back on top of the counter. "Just a little surprising is all. I've worked here since before Mr. Duskin was transferred here and in all that time I believe he's only had one other visitor."

Nolan and I share a look, and he jumps into the conversation.

"You wouldn't by chance remember who his visitor was, would you, ma'am?" he asks politely.

"Oh, heavens no!" she replies with a chuckle. "It was so long ago that the log books for that time have already been sent down to storage, otherwise I'd look it up for you. The only reason I remember is because we keep reports on which inmates receive the largest or the least number of personal visits, and every month for eighteen years, Mr. Duskin is always at the bottom of the list with just that one visitor in all this time."

She moves away from the counter, busying herself with getting our visitor badges in between answering the phone when it rings. After a few minutes, she hands us the badges and quickly runs down the list of rules we'll need to follow when they call us, such as remaining only in the designated visiting area, no talk of the prisoner's treatment or questions about his daily habits in the facility, no conversations that will anger or upset the prisoner in any way, and when our thirty minutes are up, we must end our visit immediately without any trouble or we will never be permitted back.

I'm sure we'll have no trouble following the rules, but even if we can't, it's not like I plan on coming back here to visit Tobias again anyway.

Nolan and I pin the visitor badges to our clothing and then take a seat in the hard plastic chairs pushed against the wall until our names are called.

"Do you know what you're going to say to him?" Nolan asks softly as we watch a few more people enter the building and go up to the counter to check in.

"I guess I'll just get right to the point and ask him if he knows he's my father," I reply. "That's the only question I care about getting an answer to right now."

If I had more than thirty minutes with him and if Nolan wasn't here with me, I might ask him why he killed his parents and a handful of strangers. I'd ask him if he thought about it beforehand, dreamed about it, craved it, and it just became too much, and he *had* to do it before the thoughts in his head drove him crazy. Basically, I'd ask him if that was something I had to look forward to, since we share the same bloodline.

"Visitors for Duskin?"

Nolan and I stand up from the chairs when a guard holding a clipboard announces our name. We follow him through a door leading away from the waiting area and down a long hallway, stopping in another small room. We're asked to remove any items we might have in our pockets so they can be inspected. Nolan removes his wallet and keys, placing them on the table, and we wait while another guard quickly checks them over, passing Nolan's wallet back to him and informing him he can pick up his keys after the visit.

Moving out of the room, we continue on down the hallway, coming to a closed door. The guard unlocks it and then holds it open for us. In the middle of the stark white room is a long wooden counter that runs from wall to wall. There are booths separated by wooden walls attached to the counter, two metal chairs inside each booth and a glass partition running right down the middle.

"Duskin will be in booth number eight, right down there," the guard tells us, pointing to the booth at the very end that has a sign taped to the inside wall with the number eight written on it. "When he is escorted to the booth, you can pick up the phone on your side of the counter to communicate, and he'll do the same on his side. You will have exactly thirty minutes from the time he sits down."

Without another word, he turns and exits the room. I walk slowly toward booth eight, glancing at the booths we pass, all currently occupied by other people visiting prisoners, the low hum of conversation filling the room. Nolan pulls out a chair for me and I take a seat, clasping my hands together in front of me on the counter, staring at the empty chair on the other side of the glass.

Nolan wisely keeps his mouth shut while we wait, and I tap my foot against the floor under the counter in nervous excitement that I can't even explain. I'm here to confirm whether or not my parents lied to me my entire life about who my father really is, and excitement probably isn't the most appropriate feeling to have right now, but I can't help it. What little I know about Tobias Duskin already fascinates me, and I'm anxious to find out more.

A door on the other side of the partition suddenly opens, and my eyes greedily take in the man in shackles being led to his chair across from me.

"Oh my God," Nolan whispers as the guard helps Tobias sit down in his chair, saying a few words to him that we can't hear because of the glass and then exiting back through the door, leaving us alone for our visit.

Oh my God is right. Looking at this man across from me is like looking at a more hardened version of my father. They look so much alike they could pass for twins. I watch in silence as he stares right at me, our eyes the exact same shade of green. My mother has the same color eyes as I do, so it's not really proof he's my father, but something in his eyes calls to me. I can't look away, and the glass that separates us angers me. I want to reach across the counter and touch him, grab ahold of the energy and excitement that radiates out of his stare and pull it inside of me.

I slowly lift the phone receiver and hold it against my ear, waiting for him to do the same. His eyes never leave my face and a few seconds later, he reaches for the handle of his own phone, the shackles on his wrists making him use both hands to bring it up to his ear.

Static crackles through the line for a moment, and then I hear his smooth, deep voice.

"Hello there, darlin'."

The corner of his mouth tips up in a half-smile, and my heart thumps loudly in my chest. His voice fills me with needs and wants and a feeling of power that I can't even explain.

"You know who I am?" I ask softly.

He chuckles, the sound warming my skin in the damp, chilly room.

"You look just like your mother, so it's not hard to guess who you are," he replies.

"But do I look like you as well?" I ask, holding my breath, waiting for him to confirm my suspicions.

"Could be, but you'd have to ask her that."

"She's dead, so that's not really an option," I reply.

"Let me guess: Tanner finally bored her to death?" he asks, laughing at his own joke. "My brother wouldn't know how to have a good time if it jumped up and bit him on the ass."

I stay quiet, waiting for him to keep talking. At this point, I don't even care what he says; I just want to hear his voice.

"And here I thought he kicked me out of Gallow's just because he couldn't handle knowing his wife preferred the company of a killer over him," he continues. "He didn't just need to protect Claudia from my wicked ways: he needed to protect her bouncing baby girl too."

He rests his elbows on top of the counter to lean closer to the glass between us, and my hand grips tightly to the receiver. His words make it hard to sit still, filling me with excitement and validation.

"Why did you kill your parents when you were eighteen? What made you kill all those other people you didn't even know?" I ask, unable to hide the eagerness in my voice.

"They tried to say I was insane," he replies with a shrug. "That I wasn't of sound mind, and some even said the devil made me do it."

I hang on his every word, knowing he couldn't possibly be insane. Even after years of living behind bars, he's more articulate and composed than my parents ever were.

"The devil can't make you do something when he lives inside of you, and you welcome his thoughts," Tobias says, his voice low. "I killed them because they made me angry. I didn't like their rules, and they didn't like it that I didn't follow them. Once I got the taste of it, once I finally found something that made me feel alive, I never wanted it to end. The man at the gas station pissed me off when he wouldn't let me use the bathroom. The woman walking her dog gave me a dirty look, and the teenager at the Food Mart made fun of the blood stains on my shirt, assuming I dripped ketchup on myself."

He chuckles to himself as he relives his kills, his explanation sounding more like a simple chat about the weather than about taking lives. I have so many questions, so much more I want to know. Did he stare into their eyes as they died and smile when they took their last breath? Did he sleep soundly that night because the thoughts in his head had finally been quieted? Did the first pound of the hammer into his father's skull sound like music to his ears, music that he still hears to this day?

"Tanner was a fool for thinking that keeping me away would stop what was inside of you," Tobias says with a smile. "I see it in your eyes, little girl. I can feel it in the air. You like the way it makes you feel, don't you? You need it just to breathe, and you want it just to feel alive."

My heart beats faster with every word he says, and my head nods slowly in response.

"Don't fight it, girl. Fighting it will only make it worse. Let it live and breathe inside of you until you can't hold it in any longer."

I feel the corner of my mouth tipping up into a smile, matching the one currently on the man seated across from me. My father, the cold-blooded killer.

The door suddenly opens behind Tobias, and the guard rushes back in and pulls him up from the chair. I'm not ready for our visit to be over, and I want to pound on the glass, beg the guard not to take him away. I need his voice. I need his words. I need to savor this feeling of belonging.

"You have my eyes," Tobias suddenly tells me right before the phone is snatched from his hand and slammed down onto the receiver.

I keep the phone pressed to my ear and watch him dragged away. Smiling, he stares at me over his shoulder the entire way, until he disappears from sight.

Slowly lowering the phone and hanging it up, I

rise from my chair and walk wordlessly away from the booth. I hear the scrape of Nolan's chair against the tile, and he rushes to catch up with me as the guard standing next to the door holds it open for us.

"What did he say? Did he confirm that he's your real father?" Nolan asks as I walk in a daze down the long hallway, back the way we came earlier.

"His eyes gave me chills. They were so cold and dead," he adds, grabbing the keys from the guard we left them with and moving on.

We drop our badges onto the front desk and head outside where the rain continues to fall. Running to the car, Nolan quickly opens my door and I wipe the wetness from my face when I get inside.

"My name is Ravenna Duskin. I'm eighteen years old, I live in a prison, and I have my father's eyes."

CHAPTER 19

N OLAN DROPPED ME off at Gallow's Hill with a
promise to come back once he checked on his
mother. I'm happy for the solitude after an hour of
him asking me every few minutes if I was okay. Am I
okay knowing my real father is a psychotic killer with
no remorse for what he did? Am I okay knowing my
parents lied to me about who my father is? Am I okay
that I suddenly feel normal, like the things I feel and
think make sense and have a purpose?

I'm more than okay. I'm giddy with excitement
and wish I'd had more time with Tobias. He saw
something in me. Something I've kept hidden, but

that is such a huge part of who I am that I'm choking with the need to talk to someone about it, someone who could listen without judgment. Someone who could understand.

I told Nolan I was fine and just needed time to process things, but I'd already processed them the moment Tobias opened his mouth, and I heard his voice. Now I have a reason for never feeling like I fit in with my average, boring family, other than the clothes, the hair, and the constant perfection. I have Tobias Duskin's blood flowing through my veins, and it all makes sense now.

Kicking aside one of the empty bottles of whiskey that still litter the floor outside my father's office, I walk into the spare bedroom, stopping at the edge of the bed. Lying in the middle, folded in half is a single piece of paper I don't remember being there earlier.

Snatching up he paper, I flop down on the bed and unfold it above me, resting my head on a pillow. The handwriting is immediately recognizable, and I realize it's one of the ripped-out pages from my journal.

I rush to read the words, once again feeling like I'm seeing them for the first time, having no memory of thinking them or writing them down.

It's been two weeks of this nonsense, and I've had enough. Not only was my life flipped upside down when finding out my parents had lied to me all these years, now I have to face the product of their dishonesty everywhere I turn. I don't understand the constant questions about my daily life, my family, and the prison. So many questions that I feel as if I'm going insane, reliving everything from the last eighteen years.

Why is all of this information so important? Is it jealousy because I had a normal, happy childhood? I want to feel sympathy that I obviously had such a better life, but it's so hard to do this. It's not my fault I had it better. It's not my fault this house is filled with photos of happy times and happy memories. My parents won't stop hovering, and it's driving me insane. I know they feel bad for lying, but I can't forgive them. I'm so angry that everything in those happy photos and wonderful memories has been tainted by a secret they kept hidden.

They want me to be polite and accommodating, just as they raised me to be. Show that I'm the bigger person and make the best of this situation. It's the only reason I've agreed to go exploring in the basement when my parents leave for dinner. I hate going down there, but I'll do it if it finally stops all the questions. I'll go down into the basement and fight through my fears. I refuse to be called a chicken or accused of being afraid to take chances. Just because I wear nice dresses, keep my hair perfectly neat, and behave like a proper young lady should, doesn't mean I'm scared to be adventurous. I will go down in-

to the basement, not because I was teased into it,
but because I'm tired of always being labeled as
the good girl. I'm going to prove I can be bad
too.

Crumbling the journal page in my fist, I toss it
across the room in frustration. Why was I so cryptic
when I wrote in that stupid journal? I mention how
my life suddenly changed and lies my parents told,
but I never say what the lies were. Did I find out
about Tobias before I lost my memory? Is that why I
ran out into the woods and someone tried to hurt me?
Has my mother been the guilty party this entire time?
She admitted to pushing me into the lake and apologized for her sins and weaknesses. When I found out
about Tobias, I assumed all of that talk was about her
affair with him all those years ago and never telling
me he could be my real father. Maybe her sins went
beyond that. Maybe I found out about Tobias before
that night, and she was afraid I'd tell my father. It
would explain how differently I started acting a few
weeks before. It would explain my sudden interest in
Nolan, the change in clothes and hairstyle, and the
fighting with Trudy.

Maybe my mind started fracturing before I even
ran into the woods that night. According to the
journal page I just read, my life had been turned
upside down by something. If I was still a normal,
good girl when I found out the man who raised me
for eighteen years wasn't really my father, I'm guess-

ing that would have changed everything for me. Especially if I knew about Tobias's past and the type of person he was.

"Are you okay, Ravenna? I can't even remember the last time you were in one of the cell blocks."

My father's voice suddenly fills my head, and I think back to those first few days after the accident and the day I went to see him in the cell block while he prepared for a tour. Even then, so early on, when I was still covered in scratches and bruises and still had a bandage covering the gash on my head, nothing felt right, and the things he said to me felt like lies. I pushed those feelings aside, though, and blamed them on my jumbled brain.

I run out of my room and down the stairs, holding tightly to the banister when I get to the bottom as I swing around and head to the back of the first floor. Racing through the halls, I pass by the secretary's office, and then the storage room filled with boxes of shirts, coffee cups, and other items to restock the gift shop, and I don't stop until I get to the fork in the hallway. To the left is the west cell block and to the right is the east. I turn to the right, moving past the old guard station where new prisoners were checked in before being led to their cells, and through the alcove leading right into the east cell block.

"I can't even remember the last time you were in one of the cell blocks."

I hear my father's words again, and I move silently

across the cement floor, like I did that day I decided I was tired of being cooped up in my room and decided to go on a walk around the prison. I remember feeling like his words didn't make sense because this area felt so familiar to me, especially one cell in particular. That day in this cavernous room, five stories tall of row after row of tiny rooms where killers and rapists and other dregs of society lived out their days, I glanced inside each dilapidated cell just like I do now, looking at mangled bed frames, cracked and stained toilets, and stone walls that are crumbling, leaving behind piles of rocks and dust on the floor.

Just like that day when my father told me I'd never been in this area, a particular cell halfway down the row calls to me. It beckons me closer and I have no choice but to go to it. My feet automatically stop in front of cell number sixty-six, the number etched into the top middle of the steel frame around the cell door.

"Tobias was in cell number sixty-six. Only one more six and your father would have lived in a room with the mark of the devil on it. You're lucky I'm here to make sure you never turn into him."

My vision blurs and my body sways, forcing me to hold onto the open cell door as I remember someone telling me about Tobias. I don't remember who it was but it's a male voice, and I remember hating him for speaking about my father so cruelly. I remember telling him that I had already turned into my father and there was nothing he could do about it. A sharp pain suddenly shoots through my head as I try to remember more, try to see whom I'm talking to and who told me about Tobias.

I wince, squinting my eyes as the knives stab through my skull, and blood rushes through my ears, the pounding of my heart so loud that it's a wonder it doesn't rattle the whole building. I take a few deep, calming breaths, refusing to let the pain stop me or deter me from remembering. I can't keep allowing this brick wall in my mind to slam down each time I'm right on the verge of remembering something I know is important.

Moving slowly into the dark cell, the setting sun's orange glow that shines through the huge windows behind me lights up the shadows in the small room just enough for me to see what I'm looking for—the thing that drew me to cell number sixty-six that day I was down here with my father and what pulls me forward now.

I barely register the rocks and uneven stone floor beneath my bare feet as I move deeper into the cell, until I'm standing next to the broken toilet, right in front of the back wall. The pain in my head disappears and I open my eyes all the way, my hand coming up in front of me. My fingers gently trace over the crude drawing on the wall, careful not to press too hard and chip away any of the stone and ruin it.

"The devil can't make you do something when he

lives inside of you, and you welcome his thoughts," I speak aloud softly, my voice echoing around the stone walls as I recite the words my father said to me today, and run my fingers over the satanic image he carved into the stone when he was imprisoned here.

I repeat the words like a chant, over and over, while my fingers move away from the carving of the horned figure with the forked tongue, up to the words he engraved in the stone above it.

"You will pay for your sins," I read aloud softly.

I close my eyes and turn away from the wall, pressing my back against the cold stone and then sliding to the floor. Pulling my knees up to my chest, I wrap my arms around them and feel like I'm home.

My memories no longer make me feel like they are playing tricks on me. I know they speak the truth because as I sit here, in the cell where my father spent most of his life, I know I've been here several times before. The dampness of this space, the smell of musty stone, and the coldness of the floor seeping through my shorts pushes several moments forward in my mind where I can see myself so clearly sitting in this same spot, just so I could feel closer to him.

The words I remembered being spoken to me about Tobias and his cell number prove that I knew about him long before I found his file in…my father's office. My brain stumbles over calling Tanner my father, but that's how I've always known him, and it's hard to make myself call him by anything else right now.

I want to believe that my mother was the one chasing me into the woods because it's the only thing that makes sense. It fills in most of my unanswered questions, and it gives me a plausible reason for why it happened, especially after seeing her completely lose her mind and then kill herself right in front of me.

It would be so easy to just accept it as the truth, but I can't. As I sit in Tobias's cell and revel in the familiarity of being here, that explanation still doesn't make everything click together in my head like it should. If that was the final piece of the puzzle, if that was the one thing my mind was still keeping from me, I think I would feel it, wouldn't I? Finally figuring out the truth should make every moment from that night perfectly clear in my head, but when I try to remember who I was running from, I still see nothing but a faceless figure. I still hear a voice yelling at me, but it's neither male nor female, just threats being yelled through the woods while thunder rumbled all around me.

Letting my head thump back gently against the wall, I remember the words I read in the missing journal page and know there's only one thing left for me to do. The one thing I've always known I need to do, but kept getting interrupted before it could happen. Just like this cell, it calls to me, even stronger than before now that I've read the words I wrote.

It's time for me to get into the basement, even if I

have to break down the door.

Giving myself a few more minutes of quiet, I think about Tobias's voice and how good it made me feel that he saw right through me.

"My name is Ravenna Duskin. I'm eighteen years old, I live in a prison, and the devil is inside of me."

CHAPTER 20

I SPENT SO long down in cell number sixty-six that by the time I made it back to the main hallway, Nolan had returned from checking on his mother and was knocking on the door. Something has been screaming in my head ever since I let him in that he shouldn't be here, and I shouldn't let him go down into the basement with me, but I've pushed those thoughts aside for now. I wasn't able to get the door unlocked the last time I tried, and I need him to do it for me.

Standing over his shoulder, my body vibrating with excitement like it has the last few times I've tried to go downstairs, I tap my foot impatiently against the floor, trying not to scream at him to hurry. It feels like Nolan is moving in slow motion as he uses the same hanger he used to open the spare bedroom and the one I used unsuccessfully on this door the day my father drunkenly stumbled down the stairs and interrupted me.

The click of the lock releasing almost makes me want to wrap my arms around Nolan's shoulders and kiss his cheek, but even the thought of doing something like that makes my stomach churn.

He stands up and tosses the hanger to the floor, turns the knob, and opens the door.

"It's fine if you need to go back to your mother; I can do this alone," I tell him, trying not to come right out and tell him I don't want him here, that his presence is threatening to kill my excitement. I might be a mean, twisted person deep down inside, but at least I'm not rude. He *did* just help me with something, no questions asked, and after everything he's learned about me and helped me figure out, he still isn't running in the opposite direction because it's finally hit him that my life is entirely too messed up for him.

"My mom's asleep right now, so I don't have to be back to give her medicine for a few hours. I'm not going to leave your side, Ravenna, don't worry," he reassures me, leaning down and placing a kiss on my cheek.

Just like I figured when I thought about doing it myself, the feel of his warm lips against my skin makes me feel nauseous, but I'm completely surprised that it also calms me in some way. I'm so on edge right now that I feel like I'm going to jump out of my skin. The door is finally open, and I know with everything inside of me that going down these stairs will give me the answers to everything. I don't even know how to explain what I'm feeling. I don't know how I *know* the last of the secrets are down here—I just do.

Nolan's kiss, while almost vomit-inducing, slowed my heart down, so I no longer feel like it might explode. It also stopped me from screaming at him to get the hell away from me. I should be worrying that I'm growing more comfortable with him, but I don't have time for those pointless thoughts right now. Just as I wrote, over and over, in my journal, the secrets are hidden in the walls of this prison, and I know, without a shadow of a doubt, that they are down those steps, beyond the darkness.

"Can you grab two flashlights?" I ask him, pointing distractedly to the small side table behind him and against the wall next to the basement door. "My father keeps a bunch there for tours since there's only one light at the bottom of the stairs."

I stare in a daze at the rickety wooden stairs that disappear into the blackness of the basement, so deep the lights from up here can't reach. Nolan taps my arm with the end of a flashlight and I jump, realizing he'd been holding it out in front of me while I was busy staring.

"Come on, let's go into the basement."

"Are you crazy? It's scary down there."

"It's not scary when you go with someone else. Come on, there's something I want to show you."

"I've been down there before, believe me, there's nothing I haven't seen."

"You haven't seen the bones…"

The conversation I remembered the last time I tried to go down into the basement floats through my mind, as well as the words I read from the journal page earlier. That page made it sound like someone else was making me go into the basement, but the memory of that conversation is perfectly clear in my head. I can see myself standing in this very spot, hands on my hips and a cocky smile on my face as I coerced whoever it was to come with me.

Taking the flashlight, I head down the stairs, hoping the rest of that memory will come to me when I get down there.

"Are you sure you're okay, Ravenna? You're breathing pretty hard and your hands are shaking," Nolan says softly as he follows me down the stairs.

"It's calling to me," I whisper. "I can feel it. I *need* to go down there," I whisper softly, not even caring if he hears me.

I sound crazy—I know I do—but I can't stop the words from coming out of my mouth.

"Don't go down there. You'll never come up if you go down there."

The warning my father gave me when he caught me picking the lock on the basement door suddenly feels like a bad omen, instead of the drunken nonsense of a man slowly losing his mind after the death of my mother. The words repeat on a loop in my head, getting louder and louder, until I have to press my hands against my ears to quiet them.

"Stop, stop, stop," I chant under my breath as I make myself continue moving down the stairs, the old wood creaking beneath my feet.

I don't want to hear his voice in my head. He's a liar and a fool, staying with a woman who probably never wanted him and who lied to him about my paternity. I hate him for pushing me away every time I needed him. I needed him so much, and he threw me away like I meant nothing.

"Get her away from me; I can't stand to look at her."

"She's just like him, Claudia. You can't pretend anymore. I won't let her ruin us like Tobias did."

"Look what she did, Claudia! She's only five years old, and look what she's capable of! She has to go; she'll only get worse."

"Do whatever you need to do, Dr. Thomas, just don't bring her anywhere near here again unless you can fix her."

Words I overheard long ago rush through my mind so swiftly the farther I get to the bottom of the stairs that I can barely make sense of them. Even though I've come to terms with my father's hatred toward me, it still takes my breath away to remember even more proof of that disgust and the realization that it didn't start recently. He has always hated me. He's wanted me gone since I was five years old.

"Ravenna, are you okay?" Nolan asked worriedly.

I ignore him, moving faster down the stairs until

I'm swallowed by the darkness at the bottom and my feet move off of the wooden steps and onto the cold, basement floor. I reach blindly in front of me until I feel a heavy piece of string, pulling on it until the bare light bulb in the ceiling switches on, lighting up part of the basement.

My skin tingles, not with the cold dampness in the air, but with the need to run to the other end of the basement. Each step I take deeper into this spot beneath the prison makes another brick in the wall of my mind break away and crumble to dust. I remember being five years old and already filled with anger and hatred. I remember feeling like I didn't belong in this family, and, even at that young age, I can still remember the way they always looked at me—in fear.

Nolan's hand suddenly slides around my waist and he pulls me back against the front of his body, stopping me from going any farther.

"You don't have to do this if it's too upsetting," he says softly right next to my ear. "I know you feel like all the answers are down here, but maybe we should go back upstairs and do it another time. You've had to deal with a lot lately, especially finding out you have a crazy man for a father. I'm just afraid this might be too much for you."

Wrapping my hand around his wrist that's pressed against my stomach, my fingernails dig into his skin as I pry his arm away. I keep digging and digging, squeezing and squeezing, even though he's not resisting me. I want to hurt him for calling Tobias crazy. Who is he to judge a man he only saw through a glass window and never even spoke to? Who is he to have an opinion about a man just because I made the mistake of telling him the things Tobias did that put him in prison? He doesn't know how hard it is to ignore the need, and he doesn't know what it's like to feel dead inside until you finally give in.

I feel something warm and wet beneath my fingers, and I look down to see blood trickling out of the holes my nails are making in Nolan's skin.

"Ouch!" he suddenly shouts in pain, jerking his arm away from me. "Careful with your nails, Ravenna."

He says it in a teasing voice with a hint of laughter, probably to make sure he doesn't do anything to frighten or upset the girl in front of him, who appears to be coming apart at the seams.

Bringing my hand up in front of my face, I stare at the small drops of blood that stain my fingertips, resisting the urge to lick them clean. Instead, I rub my fingers together and let it smear, the tension slowly leaving my shoulders.

I let out a slow, relaxing breath, forcing myself to calm down before I make a mistake, and Nolan leaves in disgust or fear. As much as I didn't want him down here a few moments ago, I'm glad he's here now. It's time for him to see who I really am.

"When this was a working prison, this entire area

was used for solitary confinement," I explain to Nolan, speaking softly as I begin walking again, moving slowly, deeper into the basement.

Talking puts a stop to the memories, but I'm okay with that for the time being. Too many thoughts and feelings are at war inside of me and I need a moment to quiet my mind before it all becomes too much for me to handle. I feel like I'm standing on the edge of a cliff, teetering between wanting to know everything and suddenly scared to death it'll destroy what's left of my soul when I finally remember it all. I hate being afraid. I *refuse* to be afraid, and after everything I've learned about my life so far, I know that nothing can break me. I let my knowledge about the prison and random facts roll easily off my tongue, giving me time to push aside my fear.

"It used to be sectioned off with six-by-eight foot cells made out of chain-link fence that stretched from floor to ceiling, but due to a busted pipe a few years ago, most of the cages were removed so the workers could move around easier to fix what was broken," I tell him in a monotone voice, stopping in front of one of those cells. "Now it's just one wide open, empty space with the original stone floor and crumbling stone walls, with just this one cage left for the tours."

"I feel like all we talk about is my life. You know everything about me now, including my favorite color, what I eat every day, and a bunch of other useless facts. Why don't we ever talk about you?"

"Believe me, your life is much more interesting than mine. If I told you about my life, you'd probably have nightmares. If you don't want to talk about yourself anymore, let's talk about this creepy prison. I know a few things, but I'm sure you have a bunch of good stories I haven't heard."

I pause in the middle of my explanation to Nolan when another memory I couldn't stop hits me. I can see myself sitting on the pink comforter in that awful pink room but once again, I don't know who I'm talking to, and I can't remember which part of that conversation was mine and which was someone else's.

"They were like animals in cages down here," Nolan mutters, pulling me away from my thoughts as he stares at the cage in front of us.

"Pretty much," I agree, continuing on with my story. "But you have to remember, these were for the worst of the worst. The ones who started prison riots, killed other inmates or even guards. Their punishment was being cast off into the basement, where there aren't any windows to let in sunlight and no privacy whatsoever. They lost all sense of time because it was always dark, and many of them went completely insane if they were down here for a long time. They didn't even have beds; they had to sleep on the ground. The guards back then needed to make it so awful that the men would think twice about doing anything bad again because the punishment was so severe."

"I wouldn't have to do this to you if you'd just stop being bad."

"This will only hurt for a minute. If you're a good girl, I'll tell you more stories about the place where you were born."

My chilled skin suddenly heats up like I walked into blazing inferno. My head starts to pound with a piercing headache, and even the solitary bulb that barely gives off enough light to see more than a few feet in front of us is suddenly too bright for my eyes. I squeeze them closed and press my hands to either side of my head, wanting nothing more than to make the pain go away.

This memory decides to give me everything, and I can see an older man leaning over me as he straps me to a table. His hair is the color of salt and pepper, neatly trimmed and slicked back off of his forehead. He's wearing a dress shirt buttoned all the way up to his neck, and I stare at the old, wrinkly extra skin that spills out from the tight collar of his shirt, dreaming about the day when I'm older and stronger and can slice it off with a knife. I hate him. I dream every day about killing him, and I know immediately who he is, realizing now why as soon as I heard his name from Dr. Beall, all my memories of pain were associated with him.

"I don't deserve this, Dr. Thomas. None of this is my fault, and you are going to regret this. I'll make sure you

pay for this."

"Ravenna? Are you okay?"

I hear Nolan's voice, but I can't open my mouth to speak. I'm too busy clenching my jaw as hard as I can. Pain...so much pain. It hurts everywhere and it never stops.

The electric shock waves that shoot through my body, needles stabbing up and down my arms... Forced into a tub filled with ice cubes and freezing cold water and made to sit there for hours, strapped into a straitjacket and left in a pitch-black room for days at a time... Being starved, being beaten, and so many other things that all come flooding back, making me want to scream and claw at the skin on my face and rip the hair from my head.

"Ravenna, answer me," Nolan says again, his voice finally penetrating my thoughts.

"I'm fine. Where was I?" I ask calmly, moving away from the cage and farther into the basement where it starts to get darker, the single bulb at the base of the stairs unable to provide enough light.

"Are you sure?" he asks, his voice full of fear and concern.

His fear wraps around me like a warm blanket. I want him to be afraid. I want him to be concerned for my well-being. I've taken that final step at the edge of the cliff and I'm falling so fast that no one can save me now.

The secrets are hidden in the walls of this prison.

They will destroy you before they set you free.

I chuckle out loud, thinking again about the words I wrote in my journal. These remaining secrets that are so close I feel like I can reach out and touch them can go ahead and try to destroy me. Nothing can crush me. I've lived my life in the bowels of hell, and it only made me stronger.

Flipping the switch on my flashlight, I aim the beam into the shadows in front of me, the light reaching all the way to the wall at the end of the basement. I continue walking until there's nowhere else to go.

"There's a door here, but it's camouflaged into the stone," I say robotically as my hand automatically moves right where it needs to go. "There's a room back here, but no one knows about it. It's where bad things happened. Very bad things."

"You haven't seen the bones. Didn't anyone tell you the story of the men who died down here? How do I know something about this place that you don't?"

"I should have known you'd be too scared to do it. Move out of the way; I'm not afraid of anything."

"Why am I doing this? Because they deserve to know what it feels like to lose everything. Swallow the water, breathe it in, close your eyes and just slip away. It will only hurt for a moment, and then you'll be free."

"I think we should go back upstairs," Nolan tells me as I run my palm over the cool stone wall, feeling for the doorknob. "I don't think we should open that door. Something doesn't feel right about this."

He's probably correct. Nothing good can come from opening this door, but I can't stop. I feel like I've been waiting for this moment forever and I can't turn back. The truth is right in front of me, screaming at me to keep moving, to open the door, and remember. Just remember.

"Do you remember? Do you know? T means death, death means T. Remember T. REMEMBER!"

My hand bumps into the handle, and I smile to myself as I wrap my palm around it, but pause before turning it.

"There's a story that's been passed down between the guards for years," I speak softly, letting the anticipation build before I pull the door open. The anticipating is the best part. I remember being in this room the last time. The excitement of finally coming to the end of my plan and realizing I only had one step left before it was finished.

"Behind this door is another room. There isn't much of a floor, maybe around four feet all the way around the outer edge by the wall. It drops right down into a sub-basement. I don't even know why they call it the sub-basement. It's no bigger than any other cell in the prison, but it's not a cell. It's a hole. Back in the 1800's, they didn't have solitary confinement and cages; they had 'The Hole.' Dirt floors, dirt walls, and shackles attached to those dirt walls to hold the men down there. The shackles were overkill since the hole goes down about ten feet and once you were in, there was no getting out unless the guards lowered a rope ladder."

The door creaks as I pull it open the tiniest bit.

"Something tells me this story is not going to end well," Nolan comments with a nervous chuckle, trying to lighten the moment that has clearly descended into darkness.

I ignore him and continue.

"There were four men shackled down in the hole one night when it started to rain. It came down in buckets and before they knew it, the guards noticed the hole was starting to fill up with water. Someone needed to get the ladder and go down to remove the men, but it was late. They had families and needed to make the long ride home to check on them, make sure they were safe in the storm as it pounded down all around the prison. They argued. No one wanted to go down in the hole that was filling up faster and faster with rain bubbling up from the ground. The men were screaming, begging for someone to get them out. The guards turned, made their way upstairs, and eventually the screaming stopped. The next day when the storm had passed, they went downstairs and found the hole completely filled with water, but slowly starting to drain. Still, no one wanted to go down in the hole so they left the bodies down there and closed the door."

Pulling open the door the rest of the way, I hold my breath in anticipation. There's something in this room I need to see. Something I *have* to see. It pulls me forward, moves my feet without my help and calls to me.

"So they just left four dead bodies down here. Like, forever? No wonder people think this place is haunted. This has got to be everyone's favorite part of the tour."

I shake my head, moving the beam of the flashlight along the floor at my feet, toward the room.

"This isn't part of the tour. No one is allowed in this room because my father thinks it's too dangerous. He's been wanting to have the hole filled in, but he hasn't had the time."

I finally aim the flashlight beam into the room and all the air leaves my lungs in a *whoosh* when I see what's in front of me as I continue moving inside the room until my feet are right at the edge.

A loud thunk sounds behind me and I jump, turning to see Nolan's body fall to the side, his eyes rolling into the back of his head. I cringe as his head smacks against the hard floor, my eyes slowly moving away from his unmoving form to the doorway.

With the dim light from the single bulb at the other end of the basement, I can only see a shadowed outline of the person standing in the doorway with a long, heavy piece of wood held in the air that I'm guessing is the cause of Nolan's crumpled, unconscious body lying by my feet.

I don't need a bright light to tell me who it is.

"My name is Ravenna Duskin. I'm eighteen years old, I live in a prison, and I'm going to make you see the truth."

CHAPTER 21

"**W**HAT DID YOU do? Why would you hurt him like that?" I shout, quickly glancing down at Nolan to make sure he's still alive.

Even after all the things I've learned about myself and how utterly insane I feel right at this moment as words and memories and pain and all the things I've blocked come rushing back, I still don't want Nolan to actually die, no matter how many times I've fantasized about it.

I'm realizing right in this moment, as everything starts to finally fit together in my head, that Nolan is the only thing in my life that has ever made me feel calm and normal. I will never actually *be* normal, but he makes it easier to pretend, and I think I'm starting to like it.

Seeing the slow rise and fall of his chest allows me to expel the breath I was holding and I look back to the person in the doorway, aiming the beam of my flashlight in that direction.

"I can't do this anymore, I can't. It's too much. I thought I could do it; I thought if I just acted like it never happened, I would forget, but I can't. You've made it impossible for me to forget. Nolan already knows too much: if he finds out everything, it will all be over for both of us."

My father sobs, his shoulders heaving as his arms drop and the board in his hands clatters to the ground. I watch him warily, having no idea what he's talking about and not trusting him one bit. His arm reaches out to the side and he flips a switch I forgot was there, the small room suddenly exploding with light.

"There's no point trying to go on with this charade any longer. It was a stupid idea and I should have known it wouldn't work," he tells me, his eyes darting around the room, refusing to look at me.

My frustration with him grows to epic proportions as he speaks to me with cryptic words—just like my mother did before she shot herself—instead of just spitting out what he needs to say.

"Once again, you're not making any sense. Sober up and then maybe we can talk about all the secrets and lies I've started to remember that all revolve around you," I inform him, my teeth clenched so tightly together I just might crack one in half.

"I haven't had a drink since this morning," he replies sadly. "I couldn't take another drink after I watched Nolan drive you away in my car. I knew you had been in my office, and I knew you opened the safe. The file was put in backward and the papers inside were in the wrong order. I knew where you were going, and I knew it was only a matter of time before it would all come back to you."

I look into his eyes and realize he's telling the truth. Aside from his steady clear voice, when he's not sniffling and choking back sobs, his eyes are no longer bloodshot. They're bright and filled with unshed tears, but they're clear and no longer glazed over with alcohol and grief.

"Your mother knew right away. I could see it in her eyes every time she looked at you, but she still went along with it because I asked her to. She always did whatever I asked because she knew everything that happened was because of her mistake. She would have done anything to take back that one lapse in judgment, that one moment of desire that she couldn't fight, but you can't reverse time and fix your mistakes. You just have to learn how to live with them."

I scoff, shaking my head at him, wanting to pick

up the board he dropped and smack *him* over the head so he'll start to make sense.

"Obviously she never learned how to live with her mistakes since she put a gun in her mouth and took the easy way out," I remind him.

He sobs even louder, the sound making me wince and want to cover my ears.

"I know you've started to remember the things I hoped would never come back to you. I knew it that day in your bedroom when you told me about secrets being hidden," he tells me, taking a deep breath to try and stop the quivering in his voice. "I wanted to hate you so much… You stole everything from me and still, I can't hate you. You couldn't help what you did. We tried to fix you, but we only made it worse."

An irritated laugh huffs out of my mouth and I shake my head at him in disgust. "Yes, I've started remembering things. Like Dr. Thomas and the things he did to me. Do you have any idea what I had to live through with him? And you *gave* me to him. I was five years old and you tossed me away to a sick, twisted man who got a smile on his face every time he hooked me up to the electric shock machines, stuck needles in my arms to pump me full of drugs and every other horrible thing you could possibly imagine. You wanted to hate *me*? I think I'm the one who deserves to feel all of the hate in the world for *you* and my mother."

I toss the flashlight to the side since I no longer

need it, realizing that as much as I would like to bash his head in with it, I'm still waiting for him to give me some information that I actually haven't already figured out on my own.

"You still don't remember everything, do you? Please God, remember. Don't make me relive it all over again. It's too much. Oh God, it hurts too much!" he wails pathetically.

"Don't you DARE talk to me about pain!" I shout, cutting off his mournful cries. "I spent the last thirteen years of my life, day in and day out, subjected to more pain than you'll ever know."

"Oh God! Oh God, what did you do? WHAT DID YOU DO?!"

"I gave you what you deserve. I'm letting you know what real pain feels like. How do you like it? Does it make you want to die? Or does it make you want to kill, like it does me?"

I ignore the pounding in my skull, forcing the headache away because I don't have time for it. After weeks of being confused and trying to ignore who I really was just to make my parents happy, living through nightmares and memories I refused to believe because they didn't match the lies they told me, and learning things about my life that filled me with revulsion… knowing that it was because of *them* that I didn't have any of those happy childhood memories I deserved, I want to enjoy every minute of my father finally being sober enough to listen to the things I want to say to him.

"It must be nice to have all of these happy memories and pictures to go along with them. I haven't had a birthday party since I was five. Do you remember that party? Probably not. I remember it, though, even if there aren't any photos. I guess what happened down at the lake kind of tainted the whole thing."

My hand flies up to my head, and I press my fingers as hard as I can against my forehead to stop the pain.

The photos in the living room. All those photos of a happy, normal childhood. I was in each one of those photos. I'm in each of those moments frozen in time, but I never remembered being there, even though there was proof. I don't understand. How could there be photos when I was sent away with Dr. Thomas? My childhood was filled with torture and pain, not birthdays and normalcy.

"You sent me away with Dr. Thomas when I was five," I mumble, trying to make sense of the jumbled mess of thoughts in my head.

Everything that suddenly made sense a few moments before has now become a tornado of thoughts, swirling and twisting, flashing through my mind too quickly and all wrong, blowing away before I can grab them and make them right again.

"Yes, the day after your fifth birthday. I knew

what happened at the lake was only the beginning," he explains. "You had his eyes. Even though they were the same beautiful green as your mother's, I could see it from the first moment I looked at you that they were empty and dead. Just like Tobias's when he was little. I knew you'd grow up to be just like him if we didn't do something."

I squeeze my eyes closed and shake my head back and forth.

"I never grew up here. I lived with him for thirteen years. I never came back until a few weeks ago. How are there pictures? HOW DO YOU HAVE PICTURES OF ME?!" I scream.

I hear my father sob and I open my eyes to see his knees give out as he crumples to the floor. "You have to remember. PLEASE remember. Just end this once and for all. I can't do this again!"

Backing away from him, I trip over Nolan's legs, my hand smacking against the wall to stop me from falling. I continue moving until my back hits the wall and I sink to the floor, staring at my father with his head buried in his hands as he continues to cry.

"GET ME OUT OF HERE! Why are you doing this to me? I've been nothing but nice to you! Please don't leave me down here—it's filling with water! SOMEONE HELP ME!"

"No one can hear you scream. Just like no one ever heard me scream for thirteen years."

I cry out as the pain in my head gets worse and my hands tangle through my hair close to the scalp, tugging and pulling to make it stop.

"My name is Ravenna Duskin. I'm eighteen years old, and I live in a prison," I whisper.

"STOP IT!" my father suddenly screams.

I glare at him, knowing I'm right back on the edge of that cliff. I thought I was falling before, but that was just a small jump. This time when I take that final step, I'm going to crash when I hit the bottom, breaking into a million pieces that will never fit back together.

"My name is Ravenna Duskin. I'm eighteen years old, and I live in a prison," I say again, louder this time.

"STOP IT!" my father shouts once more. "RE-MEMBER, DAMN YOU! LOOK INSIDE THAT HOLE AND REMEMBER!"

I've always hated Tanner and Claudia Duskin. I hated them for giving me away and I hated how Dr. Thomas thought it was a treat for me to hear stories about them and their lives—lives that I'd been re-moved from. He taught me about the prison and he's the one who told me about Tobias. I knew almost everything before I came back here, dead set on get-ting my revenge. My plan was in place but in order for it to work, I only needed to learn a few more things.

"Aren't we finished with all the questions? I'm pretty

sure you now know more about me than anyone else in the world."

"You're right. I think I know everything I need to about your life and the person you are. I think it's time for that trip down to the basement that you promised me."

No, no, no. This isn't right. It can't be. The walls of this prison aren't just whispering the secrets they've hidden, they're screaming the truth, and it's bleeding out of them, dripping down the stones and covering the floor. I was wrong. The words I wrote in my journal were all wrong. The walls might have seen everything, but the truth that will destroy me is really buried in the floor.

"My name is Ravenna Duskin. I'm eighteen years old and…"

My voice trails off as my eyes slowly move away from the man who continues to sob a few feet away. They move across the stone floor at his feet until they stop at the edge of the hole.

"The men are coming tonight to fill this in. Oh God, what do I do? I can't let them see this. They can't come down here. I'll just cover it up. I'll cover it up and I'll pretend like it never happened. It's okay. Everything will be okay. Ravenna is fine and everything will be okay."

I hear my father's words so clearly in my head that I have to glance back at him to make sure he isn't really speaking. I can still hear the thunder booming around the prison while he spoke like a madman, pacing around this room and making a plan I knew would never work. Ravenna would never be fine. Ravenna would never be okay and he only had himself to blame.

"My name is Ravenna…"

I can't make the rest of the words come out. They won't come out because my eyes have moved back to the edge of the hole. The hole that is no longer wide open and a danger to anyone who comes down here. I stare at the large piece of wood that covers it, knowing there was no point in my father covering it up. You can't go back in time to fix your mistakes, just like he said. Throwing a cover over it and pretending like it never happened won't make it so.

It happened. I made sure it happened and my plan was executed perfectly. I had no regrets, no remorse. It made me feel alive for the first time in my life.

"I see it in your eyes, little girl. I can feel it in the air. You like the way it makes you feel, don't you? You need it just to breathe, and you want it just to feel alive."

Leaning my body forward, I get on all fours and slowly crawl to the edge of the hole while my father's cries get louder, his wails of grief echoing around the room like the ear-piercing sound of lambs being slaughtered. My heart beats faster and I feel something stirring inside of me. The last piece of the puzzle, it's right here in front of me, and I have no choice but to grab it. I want to see. I *need* to see. I ran out into the woods in the middle of a thunderstorm because I knew he would kill me for what I'd done. He chased and he chased and he screamed and he almost did it, too.

"Oh God, Ravenna! My baby! My poor baby!" my father cries from behind me.

My hand presses against the edge of the wood and I slowly push it back, uncovering the hole inch by inch.

"I love you, Ravenna. I love you more than you could possibly imagine, and I'm so sorry. We'll be together again soon. Wait for me."

I hear my mother's words to me the night she killed herself and I didn't understand why she said we'd be together soon. It made no sense that she wanted me to wait for her in a place that she'd be going to first.

The wood scrapes against the stone floor as I continue moving it out of the way, refusing to look down until the last second, building the anticipation, letting the excitement grow until I'm ready to burst. If I lean forward any more I'll fall in, so I give the wood one big, hard shove and watch it slide across the floor until it bumps into the wall on the other side of the room.

The hole is wide open now, just a large dark pit with dirt floors and dirt walls where they used to leave men to die. It's a good place to hide secrets, but I've just proven that they never stay buried for long. The truth will always claw its way out, screaming to be heard.

"My name is…"

Sitting back on my knees at the edge of the hole, I hesitate before looking down, keeping my eyes on the wall across from me.

"LOOK, DAMMIT!" my father shrieks from behind me, his voice so shrill that it hurts my ears. "Stop repeating that nonsense and LOOK!"

I won't let his voice anger me, not this time. I do as he says one last time, following his orders like a good girl, knowing that whatever happens next, it will be the last words he ever says to me.

My eyes move slowly down the wall, across the few feet of stone floor and over the edge of the hole. They move down, down, down, over almost eight decades of packed dirt, dirt that became so hard after the natural spring beneath it continuously filled it with water over the years, whenever there was a hard rain. It's not hard enough, though, to prevent the scratches and claw marks I can see on the walls from fingernails that clawed so hard into the packed dirt that a few snapped off and are still stuck there.

"My nails are broken. Why is there dirt under them? Why are there scratches and bruises all over my arms?

What happened? Why can't I remember anything?"

"Shhhh, everything will be fine, Ravenna. You had an accident a few days ago, but everything will be fine. Just close your eyes and rest."

The thunderstorm that night came at the perfect time. My plan included other more painful and gruesome ideas that I first started dreaming about when I was five years old, but this was for the best. It's not my fault I had the excellent swimming skills and was never afraid of water. It's almost laughable that something so refreshing and cleansing, and the one thing that could make my pain disappear during sporadic rewards for good behavior over the last thirteen years, became the catalyst for someone else's pain and misery.

I failed when I was five and they sent me away.

I succeeded at eighteen, only to be chased out into the rain and hit over the head in the hopes that I would die for my sins, resolving them of theirs.

It's a pity they had to learn the hard way that you can't kill evil. Not with torture, not with guilt, not with lies...maybe it's not something anyone can physically stop. Maybe it's not something that can be bashed with a brick to the head, and it's definitely not something that can be covered up with lies when that brick doesn't get the job done, in the hopes that it won't remember the truth.

Evil always remembers the truth.

I already know what my eyes are going to find

when I get to the bottom of the hole. The tornado in my mind has suddenly ended, dropping all the pieces and parts, fragments of memories and bits of conversations into all the right slots, and I see everything now. I remember it all, and I finally have the answers to my questions.

It really is amazing how the mind works, and Dr. Beall was right. A person's mind will stop her from remembering certain things until she's ready. Until that shattered and broken mind is healed enough to finally see the truth and accept what they tried to make her forget.

I lean forward and I see.

Nothing will ever be the same again.

Nothing will ever be good again.

It will all be bad.

Bad.

Bad.

Bad.

"My name is…"

I stop in the middle of my sentence, forcing myself to hold the rest of the words in a little bit longer as my eyes come to a stop at the very bottom of the hole. Now that I can see, now that I can remember, I wait for the anticipation to build once again. When I say the truth out loud, I'll finally be free and I want to savor the excitement.

I stare at the girl with the long black hair, forever pulled into a tight braid. My eyes move over the dress that will never again be a bright shade of pink but an ugly, dull brown caked with mud and forced to dry with stains and streaks left behind by the dirty water that filled the hole. I look into the wide-open green eyes that now look just like my real father's, and mine—dead and empty.

"Do you see?" he whimpers behind me. "Do you finally remember what you did? RAVENNA! OH MY GOD, MY BABY! I LOVE YOU. I'M SO SORRY!"

He screams the name and his words of love as loud as he can and now I know he's not talking about me. Just like my mother wasn't talking about me when she apologized, told me she loved me, and begged for me to wait for her.

They never loved me. They never wanted me. It was all for *her*, the girl at the bottom of the hole, who got everything that should have been mine. She was the good one, and I was the bad one, and that's how it would always be.

I failed when I was five and tried to drown her in the lake.

I succeeded at eighteen and finally got my revenge.

"It's my turn now, Ravenna," I say to the girl at the bottom of the hole. The girl who looked just like me. The girl who had the same blood running through her veins.

The girl who was good, when I was nothing but

bad.

Standing up next to the hole, I turn around and pick up the piece of wood lying on the ground in between the two men, one still unconscious on the right, and one still sobbing into his hands on the left. I hold the wood with the rusty nails protruding from the bottom tightly in my hands and lift it above my head, trying to decide if I should bring it down to the left of me, or to the right.

Either direction will make me feel good, so it's not like it matters. The one on the left is more deserving, but it's almost more satisfying to know he'll go on living out the rest of his days in complete and abject misery. The one on the right gives me pause, but I know he'll never be able to accept the truth of what happened down here and what I did. It was nice pretending I could be normal for a little while, but I'm finished pretending.

"Ravenna, Ravenna, Ravenna," my father intones in between sobs.

"Ravenna is dead. Ravenna doesn't exist," I say with a smile.

I slowly lift the wood above my head and then quickly slam it down, knowing I made the right decision. Yanking on the wood to pull the bloody nails out of the skull resting against the floor, I open my mouth, finally setting myself free as I lift the wood again and slam the nails home.

T means death, death means T. Remember T. RE-

MEMBER!

"My name is Tatiana Duskin. I'm eighteen years old, and I will never, ever live in a prison again. I finally remember. I'm finally free."

EPILOGUE

Summer 2015

"DO YOU GET it now? Does it all make sense?" I ask, my mind exhausted, and my body feeling every bit of its sixty-eight years of age after so many hours talking.

I look back and forth between the two raven-haired beauties sitting on the loveseat across from me, mirror images of each other on the outside, but polar opposites on the inside.

"I've been asking you my entire life to talk about what happened when you were eighteen, and this is what you come up with when you're finally ready to speak? An outrageous, morbid story that is completely preposterous. Honestly, Mother, is it so hard for you to just tell us the truth?"

Faina throws up her hands in irritation, rising from the loveseat and snatching her purse from the floor by her feet, turning her annoyed look to her sister.

"How can you sit there so calmly, Mavra?" she asks.

Mavra shrugs and looks away from her sister. We

share a smile and once again I take a quiet moment to look at my forty-year-old twins. Faina meaning *light* in Russian and Mavra meaning *dark,* so perfectly named when they were born, long before I learned who they would become.

Shaking her head, Faina walks around the coffee table, bends over, and places a kiss on the side of my cheek, always remembering her manners even when she's angry. "I'm sorry, Mother, I shouldn't have spoken so rudely to you. I love you."

She stands back up to her full height, tugging the hem of her light pink suit jacket back into place and pressing her palm down the side of the matching light pink skirt. She glances down at the watch on her wrist before smoothing her hand against the side of her head, making sure her tight, perfectly pulled-back bun is still intact, and there isn't one hair out of place.

"I have to be in court in an hour, and I need to prepare. I'll give you a call later."

My beautiful Faina, the lawyer, so smart and perfect and good. It's a wonder she lived to adulthood, and I never smothered her in her sleep as a baby.

Mavra and I watch in silence as she throws the strap of her purse over her shoulder and walks out of the room, her heels clicking down the stairs as she goes. When I hear the front door open and close, I turn away from the stairs, patting the spot next to me on the couch.

Mavra gets up, walks around the coffee table and

takes a seat, turning to face me, tucking one leg underneath her.

"Aren't you going to yell at me as well and tell me my story was absurd?" I ask softly.

She shakes her head back and forth, her long, wild mane of black hair swishing around her shoulders. Reaching between us, she grabs my wrinkled hands covered in age spots and holds them in her own soft, younger ones, covered in dirt and scratches.

"You've never lied to me before; why would you start now?" she replies calmly.

My lovely Mavra, the gardener. So trusting and open, never hiding who she is or what she feels, even if society says it's bad.

I run the tips of my fingers over the new scratches on the tops of her hands and the scars from previous ones.

"Looks like you've been fighting with the rose-bushes again," I tell her with a laugh.

She chuckles with me, giving my hand a gentle squeeze. "You know I don't mind the pain. Or the blood."

"Especially the blood," I add with a smile.

We sit in silence for a few minutes and I can see it in her eyes that she still has questions.

"Go ahead and ask. I'll tell you anything you want to know."

She ponders for a few seconds, organizing her thoughts before speaking.

"You were never Ravenna?"

I shake my head.

"You were always Tatiana," she states.

I nod. "I even have the birth certificate to prove it."

"But Ravenna was real, wasn't she?" Mavra asks.

"She was. For eighteen years she was as real as you and I. I even have *that* birth certificate to prove it, but I keep that one hidden," I reply with a wink.

"You were twins, just like Faina and I."

I nod again. "Just like you and Faina. One good twin, one bad twin."

I don't feel guilty that I gave my twins the same labels my parents gave to Ravenna and me. The difference with my daughters is that they've known who they were from the moment they were born. Maybe I was always a little more honest and open with Mavra because she's so much like me, but I never made them feel like they weren't equally loved and equally cared for.

"You pushed Ravenna into the lake on the day of your fifth birthday. They never loved you, and they always made you feel like you didn't belong. Even at five years old you knew she was the good one, you were the bad one, and they'd never see you any other way, so you proved them right," she says.

I don't say a word, letting her work through it on her own.

"You failed, though. Someone jumped in and

saved her. Who was it?" she asks.

"Remember the part of the story when I met Beatrice Michaels?"

Mavra nods, and the confusion on her face disappears.

"That's right," she announces happily. "She told you she knew you'd come back and finish what you started. She said her husband pulled that little body from the lake and rescued her. So Nolan's father saved Ravenna, knew everything, and he told his wife. Even with her being so sick and all those years that had passed, she still remembered. But wait, how did no one else know there were twins? You lived there for five years. Certainly someone who worked there saw both of you."

I shake my head. "My parents knew the moment I came out of the womb. Even though Tanner saw with his own two eyes that my mother and his brother had an affair, for nine months he still held out hope that the twins she would give birth to would be his. Ravenna came out first, peaceful and cooing, looking just like our mother and they both sighed in relief. I joined them two minutes later, angry and screaming, with a crescent moon-shaped birthmark the size of a fifty-cent piece on my upper thigh, perfectly matching the one that Tobias had in the exact same spot."

Mavra's eyes widen in shock, but I continue, even though I know she still has questions.

"My father wanted to get rid of me immediately.

Maybe he wanted to kill me, maybe he wanted to give me away, but my mother wouldn't allow it," I explain. "We were both tiny, innocent babies, and she told him there was no way for them to know right then how we would turn out. *Just give it time, Tanner, please,*' she begged. He agreed, but he refused to let anyone know there were two of us, just in case. Ravenna and I were never allowed downstairs at the same time. We could never go outside and play together…only one at a time, just in case…"

Mavra closes her eyes and bows her head, processing what I just told her.

"Even though he promised, Tanner could never look at me without thinking about his brother, and, of course, my mother's betrayal. I never even had a chance. It only took five years for me to prove him right."

Mavra lifts her head back up. "So he sent you away with a horrible man the day after you pushed Ravenna in the lake. That day you looked at the photo of Tanner, your mother, and a five-year-old girl that was on the mantel, you could remember the photo being taken back then, but all you remembered was screaming and begging and being pulled away, not posing for the family picture."

My head bobs in confirmation.

"My mother forgot to cancel the family photo session that day. She'd been too upset and distraught after Ravenna was pulled from the lake and given mouth-to-mouth. My memories the day I saw that photo when I was eighteen were correct," I inform her. "Dr. Thomas was dragging me away, kicking and screaming, when they stood for the photo. Ravenna wasn't looking at the camera when the flash went off because she was watching me go."

Mavra bites her bottom lip, her face scrunching up as she thinks.

"Nolan's father told his wife about the two of you. Why didn't he tell anyone else? He worked there for years and suddenly found out there were two daughters instead of one and he never told anyone?" she asks.

"Tanner was very good at threatening people to keep his secrets. If Mr. Michaels didn't keep his mouth shut, he'd no longer have a roof over his head or a paycheck to feed his family," I tell her. "There was nothing Mr. Michaels could do but follow his orders and keep his secrets. Beatrice had already started to get sick off and on by that point, and he had a seven-year-old son to think of. He couldn't lose his job or his home."

Mavra turns away from me to stare in silence at the fireplace across the room. I let the ticking of the old grandfather clock downstairs soothe me with its rhythmic sound.

"Did you fake your memory loss that entire time?" she asks.

I laugh and shake my head.

"I was a good actress, Mavra, but not that good. When Dr. Thomas died of a heart attack, enabling me to finally get away from him, I went straight to the prison. I'd been planning that reunion ever since the day they sent me away. I showed up on their doorstep with a forged letter from Dr. Thomas announcing I'd finally been cured," I explain. "Ravenna was standing right there in the hallway and they had no choice but to tell her the truth that she'd forgotten after thirteen years—that she had a twin sister who'd been sent away when we were five."

Mavra narrows her eyes in concentration for a few moments before turning her head to look at me.

"Did you kill Dr. Thomas?"

I shake my head. "Technically, no, but I certainly didn't do anything to try and save him."

Standing above the man who tormented me for the last thirteen years, I smile as he clutches his hands to his chest, his eyes filled with fear and pain from the heart attack I assume he's having.

"Please…call…ambulance…" he stammers, gasping for air.

I walk into the hallway without a word, leaving him on my bedroom floor, where he collapsed before he could take me to the examination room for my daily round of suffering. My eyes never leave his as I lift the receiver of the phone that hangs on the hallway wall and dial 0. I keep my face blank, listening to the ringing on the other end of the line through one ear and Dr. Thomas wheez-

ing through the other. I want to laugh at the look of relief in his eyes as he watches me through the doorway, assuming I'm stupid enough to help him.

When my call is answered and I speak, I watch the expression in his face quickly change from hope that help would be on the way to wide-eyed panic.

"Yes, Operator? Could you please connect me to the taxi service?"

When I'm passed through and rattle off the address for the taxi that will arrive within fifteen minutes to take me to the bus station, I can't help but laugh as I hang up and walk back to Dr. Thomas's side.

Crouching down next to him, I chuckle again as his face turns an alarming shade of red and sweat drips down his forehead. Placing one palm against the left side of his breastbone, I feel the thump of his heart through my hand, the seconds in between beats growing longer and longer.

"Don't be a chicken, Dr. Thomas. You knew this day would come. You should have spent more time being afraid of me, instead of hurting me."

The memory of the day I finally got away from Dr. Thomas quickly fades when Mavra speaks again.

"You spent the next two weeks learning everything you could about Ravenna," she states slowly, parts of the story finally clicking into place. "You already knew a lot about the prison and their lives since you were taken away, but you needed to know more about your twin. Her favorite color, her likes and dislikes, her daily activities…you pretended to be her friend so she'd give you the rest of the information you needed because…"

She trails off, looking at me imploringly to finish the thought.

"Because my plan had always been to come back and take what was rightfully mine," I continue for her. "Get rid of the good, perfect sister and take her place. It was *my* turn to have loving parents and a good life. When she was out of the picture, I would slide right into her life and announce to my mother and Tanner that *Tatiana* left in the middle of the night and things could go back to the way they were. Unfortunately, things didn't go quite according to my plan."

What a stupid, stupid girl. I can't believe how easy it was to get her to climb down into the hole to look for bones that aren't even there. As I stare at her body floating at the top of the water that quickly filled the hole from the storm raging outside, I can't help but smile.

Watching her splash and struggle as the water continued to rise above her head was entertaining. Listening to her gurgled screams for help when the water poured into her mouth as she sank was music to my ears.

"WHAT HAVE YOU DONE? OH MY GOD, WHAT HAVE YOU DONE?!"

Tanner's voice fills the room as he rushes to the edge of the hole and looks down at Ravenna, floating lifelessly in the water that has begun to recede.

"NO! NO, RAVENNA! MY BABY, OH NO!"

I watch as he sobs for the daughter he loved more than me, pushing myself up from the floor to stand next to him.

His head whips around, and his misery suddenly turns to fury.

"I should have killed you when you were born!" he screams, spittle flying from the corners of his mouth. "You're a monster! You're the devil! I WON'T LET YOU GET AWAY WITH THIS!"

"Tanner came back to the prison early," I tell Mavra, pushing aside the memory of what happened that night in the basement. "My plan was to hide the body so they'd never know. It would have worked, too, if he hadn't forgotten his wallet at home. He left my mother at the restaurant and hurried home to grab it. He saw the basement door open and came down to investigate."

Mavra nods, continuing where I left off.

"And that explains the flashback you had when you came out of hiding, overhearing Tanner and Ike fighting about filling in the hole," she announces with a smile, pleased with herself that she's able to put it all together. "Tanner threatened to kill you, and you ran out of the basement and hid until you could come up with another plan."

I nod. "It might have worked if Ike hadn't seen me in the hallway. When I showed up at the prison two weeks earlier, Tanner put him in charge of keeping an eye on me. He didn't know what I'd done to Ravenna, but he knew something was up. When I ran out the front door, he yelled down to Tanner and told him I was running away. Tanner chased me into the woods and hit me over the head with a rock. He thought he'd killed me and it was all over."

Mavra crosses her arms and cocks her head to the side. "But Nolan was in the woods and carried you back to the prison. When you woke up confused and missing memories, Tanner decided to pretend you were Ravenna. Without even knowing your plan, he put it into action, telling your mother that Tatiana tried to hurt Ravenna and then ran away. He figured if they just kept telling you that you were Ravenna, you'd be too confused to question it, but your mother knew something wasn't right."

She pauses for a moment, looking at me in confusion. "But what ever happened to Ike? No one saw him again after that night?"

"Tanner liked to think I was the monster in the family, but he had his own evil lurking inside of him," I tell her with a sigh. "After he hit me over the head, he turned to go back to the prison and found Ike watching him. He couldn't let anyone know what had happened, so he killed him. He took the rock that was still in his hand, covered in my blood and he bashed Ike's head in."

Mavra shakes her head in awe and lets out a deep sigh.

"Why do you still keep the newspaper article about that last night hanging on the fridge?" she asks.

"Are you kidding me?" I reply with a laugh. "I'm quite proud of that article. Do you have any idea how hard it was to come up with a believable story so quickly?"

She shakes her head and rolls her eyes good-naturedly.

"I really have no idea how you did it. Not only did you have to hide the dead body of your twin sister at the bottom of the hole, you also had to explain the dead body on the floor filled with nail holes and gushing blood."

I take a moment to go back in time and remember that night. I wasn't scared or remorseful; I was just happy that I could finally breathe. I always knew I'd made the right decision that night, even if I had a moment of hesitation. I knew when Nolan woke up and learned the truth, he would never understand and never be able to accept who I was.

Still holding the piece of wood in my hands, I let out a deep, satisfying sigh as I wipe a few specks of splatter blood off my cheek. I stare down at the mess I've made, wishing I could take a picture and frame it. Another shrill cry echoes around the room, followed by a gasp of pain. The wood clatters to the ground and my head whips in the direction of the noise. I quickly formulate a plan and muster up some tears before I rush to his side, dropping down on my knees.

"Oh thank God! Oh Nolan, I was so scared he killed you," I cry as I wrap my arms around him and help him sit up.

He moans again in pain, pressing his hand to the back of his head, quickly pulling it away to stare at the bright red blood that coats his palm.

"What the hell happened? I remember walking in here and you were telling me a story," he speaks in between groans of pain. "Something about guys who died down here in the 1800's. I don't remember anything after that."

Wrapping my arms tightly around his waist, I help him stand and watch as his eyes land on Tanner's body behind me, blood dripping down the side of his face and pooling on the floor by his mouth.

"What the hell? Oh, no! Ravenna, oh my God, what happened to him?" Nolan cries.

I scrunch up my face in fake distress, forcing the tears I've gathered in my eyes to drip down my face.

"Oh Nolan, it was awful! Tanner is the one who hit you over the head. He went crazy, Nolan, absolutely crazy," I sob, adding a few sniffles for good measure.

"I was so worried about you, and then he came at me, trying to get me to fall into the hole," I tell him. "I thought I knew everything, but I was wrong, Nolan. We were both wrong. I moved away from him, but he just kept coming at me, screaming the truth and telling me everything."

Nolan wraps his arms around me, turning me away from my father's body.

"Shhhh, it's okay. Everything's okay now. Don't look at him—just look at me," he whispers soothingly.

It's suddenly easy to make the tears fall because I'm upset and frustrated. I don't want to stop looking at Tanner's dead body. I want to stare at it and laugh at it and maybe kick it in the stomach just because I can.

"It's so much worse than we ever thought, Nolan. I managed to get past him and I grabbed the piece of wood he dropped. I didn't mean to do it, I swear. He was going to kill me! Oh God, he was going to kill me!" I cry, pressing my face into his chest, finally being able to smile now that my face is hidden.

Nolan rubs my back, moving both of us away from the hole and out of the room. I sigh in relief that he did exactly what I hoped he'd do, instead of going to the edge of the hole and looking down.

"I'm getting you out of here," he tells me as we make our way through the basement and up the stairs. "I'll call the police as soon as we get upstairs. You can tell me everything while we wait for them. I need to check on my mother, but I don't want to leave you."

When we get to the top of the stairs, I move out of his arms and slide my hands into his.

"I'll be fine now that I'm up here, I promise," I reassure him, swiping away my tears and putting on a brave face, knowing I'd make a great actress in Hollywood. "I'll call the police while you go check on your mother."

He hesitates and stares down at me, his face filled with worry.

"Nolan, I'm okay now, I swear. I would never for-

give myself if you stayed here and something happened to
your mother," I tell him with a perfect sad shake of my
head.

"I don't even know how long I've left her alone.
She'll probably need to eat and take her medicine, and
then I'll need to sit with her until she falls asleep to make
sure she digests everything okay," he explains.

"It's fine. It will take the police a while to get all the
way out here anyway. I'll go upstairs and rest on the
couch until they get here. Take your time. I'll be fine," I
reassure him.

With a quick kiss to my cheek, he turns and races
down the hall to the front door. He gives me one last
questioning look over his shoulder before he walks out the
door.

"Go, I'll be okay," I tell him.

As soon as the door closes behind him, I turn and run
as fast as I can back down the stairs into the basement.

"You really are an evil genius," Mavra says with a
laugh, pulling me from my memories. "I can't believe
you were able throw a bunch of heavy stones into the
hole to keep her weighted down, drag a hose over to it
and fill it with enough water to cover the body."

Turning my head to the right and looking into
the kitchen, I smile when I see the old, faded newspaper article held up with a yellow smiley face magnet.

"Brave eighteen-year-old woman endures nightmare and lives to tell the tale," I say aloud.

My eyesight doesn't let me see much farther than

a few feet in front of me, but I don't need to see the title of the article to repeat it.

"Now you know why I kept the article all these years," I tell her, looking away from the fridge and back at my daughter. "It's not like I could go around telling people I'm an evil genius, so I wanted to make sure I'd always have a reminder."

I'm treated to another eye-roll from Mavra.

"Even though I've read that article so many times over the years, now that I know what really happened, I am completely amazed. You were able to explain away everything so the police wouldn't convict you of murder, and you gave Nolan something he could believe and something he would understand," she states. "They all believed you really did have a twin sister and her name was Ravenna, allowing you to move forward using your real name of Tatiana. They even believed she died when you were both five years old from drowning in the lake. And on top of that, with Nolan's statement confirming your parents' strange behavior toward you in recent weeks, they even believed that your parents were so distraught over the death of their daughter Ravenna that they spent the next thirteen years trying to turn you into her, pretending like it never happened. Complete with electric shock therapy to make you forget you had a twin."

I smile, happy that my daughter acknowledges just how much trouble it was to come up with all of that, while at the same time trying to hide my sister's dead body so it would never be found.

"Don't forget, Tanner *supposedly* found out two weeks before my accident in the woods that the twins his wife gave birth to eighteen years prior weren't really his, but the product of an affair she had with his brother, who was locked in a cell in his own prison, right under his nose," I add, reciting more of the article.

"That's right," Mavra replies. "A perfect explanation and one that Nolan could once again confirm for the police, to explain why you started acting so differently two weeks before the night in the woods and why your father suddenly behaved as if he hated you."

"And then of course we have the night in the woods, when Nolan found me bleeding from the head, on the ground during a thunderstorm," I continue. "Tanner, already a little off kilter after years of trying to make one daughter take the place of a dead one, lost his mind when his wife admitted the truth and chased me out into the woods. The police wanted to know why he did it, but I just cried and cried. I couldn't tell them why. I didn't know if he meant to kill me or just hurt me because he was so angry. And I'd never know since he was dead. Oh God help me, my whole family is dead. I never meant to kill him; you have to believe me, Officers! He was just angry, and he wouldn't stop coming at me, and I knew if I didn't do something, he'd push me right down into that water-filled hole!"

I wail, wiping fake tears from my cheeks as Mavra slowly claps her hands together.

"Bravo, Mother, bravo," she commends me.

She grows quiet again, and I watch the smile fall from her face.

"Just ask, Mavra. Whatever you're thinking, just ask," I remind her.

She blows out a breath, her loose lips making the sound of someone blowing a raspberry.

"I know you said you would never lie to me, but did you tell us the truth about our father?" she whispers.

I've always wondered why this question has never come up before, from either of my girls. I was honestly shocked that they took my explanation as gospel and just accepted it. I pat Mavra's knee comfortingly, feeling bad that she's probably held this question in for thirty years, my decision to finally tell them everything today the only reason she's finally asking it. I could give her the truth she's seeking and hope that it wouldn't make her hate me or look at me differently, or I could stick with what I told them when they were ten years old, even if it's selfish of me.

"Yes, everything I told you about your father was true," I confirm. "I tried, I really did, Mavra. I tried for ten years to have a normal life and be a normal person, hiding the biggest part of myself from my husband, and it just became too much for me. It's true that he left and never looked back when I asked him to go, but don't blame him. Don't ever hate him for leaving. He was a good, kind man and a wonderful father to you and Faina. His only fault was always doing anything I asked of him, even if that meant leaving his daughters behind."

Mavra lets out a relieved sigh, and I reassure myself that I did what I had to do. The truth would only hurt her.

"Tell me again," I ask, standing in the kitchen with my hands clasped together behind my back.

Nolan stops making a sandwich and turns to face me. "Again? Aren't you getting tired of hearing this?"

He laughs, wiping his hands on his jeans before walking across the kitchen to stand right in front of me.

"We've been married for ten years, Tatiana. You lived through hell and came out stronger than I would have ever believed. You gave birth to our two gorgeous girls, and you took over running Gallow's Hill all by yourself. You've survived all of this and still, you never believe what I tell you."

He smiles down at me, letting me know he's not mad at all that I'm asking this question again for probably the hundredth time. Nolan reaches up and brushes a lock of hair away from my face and I clench my teeth, forcing myself not to cringe at his touch.

"Please, one last time, I promise," I tell him as I stare up into his blue eyes that shine down on me with so much love and devotion that it's almost hard to believe.

He brings his hands up and holds my face in his hands.

"Only if you ask," he whispers softly.

"Tell me when you first fell in love with me," I whisper back.

Nolan replies immediately and without hesitation. "I fell in love with you the first moment I saw you, stuffy dress, pulled-back hair, snobby attitude, and all. I spent two years loving you from afar and it was the best thing I've ever done."

I close my eyes and sigh, feigning relief. I've asked him this same question since I was eighteen years old and his answer has never changed. I've tried so hard to be a good wife to him. I've tried so hard to make this work and have a normal life, but it's just not possible. I can't live like this anymore.

Nolan's answer to my question will always be the same, and I'll always wonder if he loved Ravenna more than me. She's the one he saw on his first day of work. She's the one he loved from afar for two years, not me, even though my carefully constructed lies have led him to believe it was me the entire time.

If Ravenna was alive today and he knew us both, would he still pick me?

I can't live with unanswered questions. I always have to know the truth, and this is a truth I'll never learn.

I open my eyes and smile up at my husband. My stupid, clueless, gullible husband. I say a quick apology in my head to Faina and Mavra, grateful that they are at school all day today.

"Close your eyes, Nolan, I have a surprise," I whisper softly.

He does as I ask, just like always, his blue eyes disappearing beneath his eyelids, a smile frozen wide on his face.

"I tried, I really did," I whisper too softly for him to hear.

Taking a step back from him, I move my hands from behind my back and lift the hammer over my head.

"Thank you for telling me the truth about Dad," Mavra says, filling the silence in the room and once again pulling me out of my memories.

"Always, my love. Always," I reply, still wondering why she has a confused look on her face.

"Why do I have to keep reminding you to just spit it out, Mavra?" I ask with a laugh.

She lets out a deep sigh.

"I swear this is the last thing. I just don't understand it yet. Your mother gave birth to twins, both of them from a man who wasn't her husband. How could they love one so completely and hate the other so much?" Mavra asks. "Just because of a silly birthmark?"

This is the part I've been waiting for since I finished my retelling of history to my daughters. I knew Faina would never believe it, and she'd leave in a huff, and I knew it wouldn't bother me. It didn't matter if she believed me, because I knew Mavra would, and I knew she'd ask all the right questions.

"Science has come a long way since 1965, my love. Still, after that night in the basement, I went back to see Tobias. I visited him as often as I could," I tell her, a smile lighting up my face when I think about all the conversations we had over the years behind a piece of glass, never being able to hold his hand like my daughter is holding mine right now. "Even though I knew in my heart he was my father, I'd spent too many years with unanswered questions, and I refused to live like that ever again. I had to know the answer to that final question. Luckily in the early 1960's, paternity testing became highly accurate. I asked Tobias to take a blood test and he agreed. It took several months to get the results, but they confirmed what I'd always known. Tobias Duskin was indeed my real father."

I can see the awe on my daughter's face in her wide, excited eyes and the way her lips form into the shape of an *O*. If she's this enthralled by a simple blood test, the final bit of information left will certainly make her head spin. My hands shake with excitement, but I wait. I let the anticipation build, and I savor the moment until she asks the final question.

"Okay, I know you explained that the birthmark was the reason Tanner couldn't make himself love you, but I'm still confused," Mavra says.

The thrill is almost too much for my old heart to take, but I know it will be worth the wait.

"I'm still not understanding why they kept Ra-

venna and gave you away to be raised and tested and
tortured by a man who thought he could rid you of
your evil thoughts," she says, the frustration growing
in her voice. "Even if you pushed her into the lake,
even if they thought that meant you'd turn out exactly like Tobias, how could they be certain Ravenna
wouldn't eventually end up the same way? How could
Tanner love her, cherish her and never see his brother
looking back at him in her eyes and not feel the same
betrayal he did when he looked at you?"

I close my eyes and take a deep breath, savoring
the moment, letting her stew a few minutes longer
with her confusion. Opening them again, I smile and
finish my explanation.

"Have you ever heard of the word *superfecundation*?" I ask.

I know Mavra is highly intelligent, even if she
went backpacking across Europe, instead of going to
college and law school like her sister. I know she's
incredibly smart even though she spends her days out
in the yard, instead of arguing cases in a courtroom.
I've spent forty years constantly being amazed by both
of my girls and maybe just a tad jealous that they are
so much smarter than I ever was at their age. It's nice
to finally know something she doesn't know.

After a few minutes of deep concentration, Mavra
finally sighs in annoyance and shakes her head. "I
have no clue what that is, and I've never heard of it
before."

I pat the top of her hand in sympathy. "Don't feel

too bad. I'm sure we could count on one hand how many people in the world know what that word means."

Sitting in the same spot for so long made my bones and joints ache, so I shift my body into a more comfortable position, turning to face Mavra and leaning my shoulder against the back of the couch.

"Did you know I still have a box in the attic with a few of Tanner and Ravenna's personal items?" I ask her.

"You might have mentioned it one time. I think I needed a photo of my grandmother for a school project when I was little and you took me up there to get it," Mavra remembers.

"I don't even know why I kept some of the things I did. I probably just grabbed random items to pack away and trashed the rest of them," I muse. "I never realized at the time that the things I packed away would come in handy many years down the line when so many new and incredible advancements in science would be invented."

Mavra hangs on my every word and I make sure to draw it out so I can receive as much satisfaction out of this that I can. I'm sixty-eight years old and I take my thrills where I can at this point, even at the expense of my daughter's temper.

"Even though DNA testing has been around since sometime between the late 70's to mid 80's, it wasn't something you could easily request unless you were with law enforcement," I explain. "Somewhere around 2008 this nifty little test was invented where you could send hair samples to a lab for DNA results. Would you like to know the items I just so happened to still have packed away in a box in the attic in 2008?"

Mavra keeps her mouth tightly closed, even though I'm sure she already knows the answer, allowing me my moment.

"Ravenna's pale pink hairbrush and Tanner's dark brown one," I finish with a smile.

Mavra's mouth opens and closes like a fish gasping for air. "Okay, but what does that have to do with supercala…whatever that word was you said and why would you need another DNA test when you already got the blood test results that Tobias was yours and Ravenna's father?"

Pulling my hands out of hers, I fold them together in my lap.

"*Superfecundation* is the fertilization of two eggs from two different sperm donors. There haven't been too many documented cases and the ones that were made public always resulted in fraternal twins, not identical twins."

I pause and wait for it to fall into place.

"Do you get it now? Does it all make sense?" I whisper, repeating the same questions I asked when I finished telling the girls my story.

"Oh my God," Mavra mutters. "OH MY GOD!"

Her voice grows louder and I can't help but laugh.

"I just…OH MY GOD!" she yells again.

Raising my eyebrow, I let her be the one to finish it. I've had enough fun for the day.

"Tobias was *your* father and *Tanner* was Ravenna's," Mavra says, shaking her head back and forth in awe. "You probably really were fraternal twins, but since Tanner and Tobias looked exactly alike, even with the two-year age difference, you were born identical, with the exception of your birthmark."

I watch as Mavra drops her head to the back of the couch and stares up at the ceiling.

"I think my mind is officially blown," she mutters.

I laugh, shifting my body away from her and rest my head on the back of the couch, just like my daughter.

"You know, you lied about one thing," she says, still staring up at the ceiling.

Turning my head, I study her profile in confusion. She quickly does the same and now it's her turn to smile.

"Your name is Tatiana Duskin, and you STILL live in a prison," she says, her smile growing wider until she bursts out laughing.

Proving her point, the doorbell downstairs chooses that moment to chime.

Mavra pushes herself up from the couch with a sigh, holding her hand out to help me up.

"I can't believe you're still giving tours of this place," she says as we walk out of the living room in the family quarters of Gallow's Hill and down the stairs.

"Where else was I going to go after my family was gone?" I ask, taking my time down the stairs so I don't fall. "Besides, I was able to recite the history of this place backward and forward by the time I was ten. It was a fun little exercise Dr. Thomas made me do in between shock therapy sessions."

When we get to the bottom, Mavra slides her hand through the crook of my arm and we walk to the door together. Pausing before I open the door and greet the group of tourists, I turn to face her, resting my hands on her cheeks.

"I love you, Mavra Michaels, my perfectly bad, beautiful daughter," I tell her, leaning forward to place a kiss on her forehead.

"I love you too, my crazy, amazingly bad mother," she replies with a smile when I pull back from her.

"Tell that husband of yours his mother-in-law says hello. It seems a little strange that I haven't seen him in a few months."

The corner of her mouth tips up in a cocky smile, so much like my father's and exactly like mine.

"Funny, I haven't seen him in a few months either," she replies with a casual shrug. "Make sure you check out the yellow rosebush on the south side of the property. They are growing like crazy. Must be that new fertilizer I used."

Mavra gives me a wink before opening the front door.

"Hello, welcome to Gallow's Hill! My name is

Mavra and I'm the head groundskeeper. This lovely lady will be your tour guide," Mavra announces, pointing in my direction. "Her name is Tatiana Duskin. She's sixty-eight years old, and she lives in a prison."

The End

Parts of *Bury Me* are loosely based on the history of the Ohio State Reformatory. If you would like to check out this historic prison online, or stop by for a visit if you're in the Mansfield, Ohio area, you can check it out here:

Website: http://www.mrps.org/

Facebook: http://on.fb.me/1TVsHcv

Acknowledgments

Thank you to my husband, James. You believed in this story right at the moment I first began to ramble incessantly during our prison tour, and I didn't shut up for the next two weeks. Thanks for pulling all-nighters, reading chapters as I wrote, screaming at me for only sending one at a time, and talking me down from the ledge when I cried for three hours straight. Thank you for loving me, thank you for supporting everything I do, and thank you for being my biggest fan.

A dedication of thanks will never be enough for Stephanie Johnson and Michelle Kannan. Thank you for always being there with support and threats to anyone who dares not to like something I wrote! I love you more than words can express and I am blessed to call you my friends.

A great big thank-you, hug, and promise of giving you my firstborn (don't worry, she does laundry and dishes) to Aleatha Romig for being the best cheerleader in the world and helping me after I finished with my crying fit. Thank you for the advice, shoulder to cry on (scream, curse, yell, etc.), and for welcoming me to the dark side.

Thank you to all the fans who followed me on this crazy journey and always allow me to listen to the voices in my head!

A HUGE thank-you to Erick Olic and the rest of the workers at the Ohio State Reformatory. Our private tour is the main reason this story finally came to light after two years of thinking about it. Thank you for helping me bring it to life, and for giving me special access to the prison for photos!

Last, but not least, thank you to my photographer Delia D. Blackburn and my model for the photo shoot, Karolina Galuszynski. You brought this story to life in a way I never could have imagined!

Made in the USA
Charleston, SC
30 December 2015